I0747946

Joseph Street Digest

VOLUME 5

Written by Seth Underwood

Illustrated by Matthew Childers

Joseph St Digest Volume 5
Joseph Street Digest Volume 5
JSD Vol 5

First printing edition 2023 in United States

Joseph Street Digest, an imprint of AEM Services
PO Box 10929
Rockville, MD 20849
www.josephstreetdigest.com

ISBN-13: 978-1-7379651-1-4 (paperback)
ISBN-13: 978-1-7379651-0-7 (e-book/EPUB)
ISBN-13: 978-1-7379651-2-1 (e-book/Kindle)

Contents

List of Illustrations

Introduction

Seth Underwood, Author

Seth Underwood is an eccentric author who writes dark speculative science fiction mixed with fantasy elements, usually dealing with androids, the future and angels. He's also an old table-top gamer and has some videos posted on YouTube. He currently writes for Invisible Illness and data-driven fiction on Medium.

He's been married for 25 years, which is unusual for an autistic, and has three children. His current project is a series of stories featuring events involving the crisis from the melting of the ice caps because of global warming affecting the United States and the world.

You can follow him on his Facebook page at @seth.underwood, read his freemium short stories at www.sethunderwoodstories.com, and follow him on Medium at sethunderwood56.medium.com.

Matthew Childers, Illustrator

Matthew Childers is a Tennessee based comic book artist, illustrator, and writer. Matthew has worked for Dynamite Comics, Nickelodeon, deCoubertin books, Adventures In Pulp, and is working on the upcoming Action Lab Comics fantasy adventure series Moon Hunters – Tales of the River Folk.

Seth Underwood's
Future Human Follies &
USRM-ISB Installments

Both the Future Human Follies and USRM-ISB Installments presented in this digest are but a sample of Rosella Tolfree's World. A period encompassing multiple ages of Earth from shortly after the current modern age through early space colonization. Seth Underwood set the stories in the United States, during a time where no single candidate captured the needed majority in the Electoral College for forty years; the House of Representatives elected all U.S. Presidents at the end of every term during this forty-year period. These initial installments in this digest follow Special Agent Rosella Tolfree during her early days with the Investigative Services Branch (ISB) of the U.S. Ranger Marshals, a new paramilitary organization under the National Park Service.

Rosella Tolfree's world is complex and uses complicated technologies and sciences. It's filled with injustices and racism that are leftovers from today's age, despite major social attempts to correct them. Cloning efforts have done nothing but reignited society's subtle emphasis on racial categorizing of people.

Those words, phrases, and ideas will be bold italicized, and you will find their definitions or explanations in the Glossary of Terms, People and Places (which has been placed at the front of this book for ease and convenience to the reader).

There are additional installments published in various places on the internet such as Seth's blog site, on Seth's Medium page, as well as smaller pieces on www.rosellatolfree.com. Other stories can be found on the E-JSD on Substack. These are Rosella World Stories that are about individuals living at various points of time before Rosella. You can find the same on the Rosella Tolfree website, where Seth has published extensive background information about his world.

GLOSSARY OF TERMS, PEOPLE, AND PLACES

1861 Corwin Amendment, also known as the Slavery Amendment, was adopted by Congress in 1861 but has never been ratified by the states that banned slavery. If ratified, it would allow the states to adopt the rights of slavery ownership without federal interference. Because Congress passed the amendment back in 1861, it lacks an expiration date and thus is still possible for ratification. Before Rosella's time, there were legal questions on how such an amendment would be implemented with due respects to the Reconstruction Amendments of the 13th, 14th and 15th that provide freedoms to once enslaved African Americans. This gets resolved in Rosella's time by Congress adopting a modification to the Corwin Amendment allowing the 13th through 15th amendments only to apply to those states that don't allow slavery. The whole deal was an underhanded dealing of politics during a time of crisis in the United States by Abby Mays, a House Representative from Georgia who switched parties from the Sandford Party to Democrats to get elected.

A-3 and A-4 androids. The development of the A-4 units was originally preceded by the A-1s, A-2s and A-3s. Each of these stages was an attempt to resolve various human interface issues, including simulation of appearance down to integrating the A.I. *emoware* technology itself in the A-3s. Initially, the A-1s were sexless, but by the A-2s the female form was chosen as the model form for the A series. This was a marketing decision associated with a lower human fear reaction. Now with the A-4s creation, the pinnacle of the android female form has been reached with the ability to birth a human clone from sampled DNA. The A-4s represent a complete female human replacement theory which has been helpful in space colonization. Majority of space colonization seems to have been male human dominated. Not that women have not played a role in space exploration, but the number of actual women in space and colonization projects has been proportionally small in comparison. Thus leaving Earth with a higher density of human women. It is not uncommon for Earth-side to see more women actually in charge of governments, and various other corporate functions. In short, human Earth women are enjoying a utopia of control never experienced before with the low density of men on Earth. So goes the idea that marketers claim.

Absolute power spectral density is a calculation that determines the actual power of the EEG signal.

Achim is a word means "constructed by God" as in the angels. Maybe fallen in this case.

Adriel means "follower of God."

Afro-Euromerican skin tone is a reference to a specific genetic set that became popularized after implementing the Minority Race Economic Adjustment Amendment in the United States. Scientists designed it to both provide inherent protection to increasing ultra-violet radiation because of global warming and allow people to take advantage of the Amendment's social advantages through including certain genetic markers used for implementing the Amendment. Those with the genetic set have a skin tone that is a medium or warm brown hue with yellowish undertones. Some individuals may have African facial features or curly hair, but not always as these features can be edited. Early adopters of this genetic set had been white elites for their cloned children, earning it a certain amount of social disdain, but later the set became used more so because of government encouragement as a form of public health. This notation differs from those known as Black, which are denotes naturally sourced African American genes and not the genetic created one.

Akumu is a reference to humanity as the word means formed by God from earth.

ASD is autism spectrum disorder.

A-Wi-Fi means advance wireless fidelity. Technically, a marketing term, like Wi-Fi itself, is a set of both network protocols and mobile networking. A-Wi-Fi takes care of issues that were plaguing more advance forms of generation mobile networks like 5G interfering with weather mapping and prediction. Scientists did this through a greater understanding of the quantum states of electrons and how radio signals propagate. As a result, the Social Media Net even in Rosella's time is filled with individuals making claims how this form of electromagnetic radiation is destroying human DNA and mental state at a quantum level. One of the most popular circulating conspiracy theories during Rosella's time is that late 20th century and early 21st century increasing obesity rates were caused by the increasing use of low-level electromagnetic waves emitting products, like cellphones, that caused metabolic syndrome. And that's why the Federal government has continued the rationing program after the Great Melt.

C-EEG is Continuous EEG, which is a prolonged version of an EEG.

Clone, in Rosella Tolfree's world, doesn't mean an exact copy of a person. There are two kinds of clones; Asexual clones which are clones made from one set of parent genes, and eukaryotic clones, where the DNA is sourced from two sets of parent genes and recombined. Asexual clones are inferior compared to eukaryotic clones because of the amount of available DNA information for the recombination process, which lowers possible errors. All DNA is modifiable during the cloning process to allow the parents some latitude of changes, such as eye color or sex. The cloning process automatically eliminates 99.9% of genetic defects and anomalies. About 15% of the 0.1% of clones may still develop "latent mental illness traits" which, when caught, would cause them to be placed in a special government group house for life. Not all people use this technology for human reproduction during Rosella's time, but most do.

Cotton is a street reference to a future drug developed by Dr. Daisy Miles, called boutcyclidine, a PCP analogue. It's highly addictive and a popular drug known to cause paralysis. It requires the smoking of cotton balls with the drug in it. Initially, people used regular cotton balls, but later people rolled cotton balls into cotton joints. But by Rosella's time, cotton cigarettes had been in mass production using cotton soaked with the drug.

Dr. Koremori Arai is a Japanese professor credited with many advances in quantum computing discoveries regarding artificial intelligence and cybernetics.

Dump Pouch is an expanding, or non-expanding hollow pouch traditionally used to stow your empty magazines during reloads.

Emo-Ware is short for emotional firmware. Android manufacturers added it into the A.I. brains of the A-3 and A-4 models to provide human-like emotional reasoning. A guessing system based on what the brain knows. The one drawback to the technology was the earlier A-3 implementation making them "moody." They stabilized this in the A-4s with minor changes to the algorithms.

Infopad or tactical infopad is a cross between a tablet and smartphone. Tactical infopads are a much larger pad used in military and police work, along with any industry demanding on site robust computer power, like a construction site.

Navakalesen is a word reputed to mean Americans.

NT is neurotypical. This is person who does not have ASD.

President Veronica Simmons became first the Vice President of the United States under President Rick Garrett's term when his Vice President Daryl Parsons died in office. Both Chambers of Congress confirmed Veronica as per the 25th Amendment Section 2. Her confirmation was not an easy one and only got passed by a two vote win in part thanks to pushes by the Sandford Party. President Garrett chose Veronica Simmons to help solidify his politic base among some very far right and the extremist politically viewed Americans who felt the Presidency had drifted away from them. She had little political background and was pulled right out of the Social Media Net because of the popularity of her talk show fan base with these fringe groups. It helped with her media numbers. She later became President after Congress removed President Rick Garrett from office because of an impeachment. As POTUS, she was extremely reckless and only focused on her own popularity. She ran the White House as if her Social Media Net show hadn't ended. She would resign from the office under mysterious circumstances and her whereabouts are unknown. There is no memorial library for her. One item that has surfaced on the Social Media

Net after departure, but is considered a conspiracy, is that she was a member of a little-known political party called the *Soviet Republican Front (SFR)*.

Quantum Tunneling Carrier Waves are a form of advance radio wave communication which use the tunneling aspects of quantum mechanics to project a radio wave from one point to another. An exact end position is needed for such transmission to occur to allow for the wave function to collapse. The other form of quantum communication method used in Rosella's world are Entanglement Transceivers. But these devices are bulky, used for long distances in space, and require to be super cooled.

Sandford Party took its name from the last name of the slave owner in the SCOTUS 1857 Dred Scott case. The landmark decision that said those of African descent were not citizens of the U.S. The idea was to be a statement concerning slavery, but it works against them with the more educated about certain landmark cases. As androids were being developed, people feared the loss of jobs to them. Thus the Sandford Party was born. There's no single founder as the group came together from a loose collection of like-minded individuals across the Social Media Net. Its chief aim is the reversal of the 13th Amendment seen as the problem. The basic argument goes if human slavery is allowed again, then the robots will not be needed. And since corporations are people (2010 Citizens United v. Federal Election Commission (FEC)), they can own slaves. There are many well-to-do business leaders and economists who have argued that slave ownership could have tremendous economic benefits socially, and that it doesn't have to be the "cruel." So this movement is all about a gentler and more peaceful form of human slavery, not the abusive ways of the past. They just see it to ensure that the economic need for droid workers is not needed. Because of its views on slavery, the Sandford Party has found many radical elements bounding themselves to the group, like the KKK.

Second Age of Humanity, this is referring to a human time period based on two basic axioms: 1. The conquest of a specific area of space, and 2. The ever-increasing life span of humanity to deal with this conquest. There are currently Six Ages of Humanity, with the one we are living in being the First Age. The Rosella Tolfree stories take place in later half of the Second Age.

Shuchah is a word that means pit.

Skin-walkers is an Indigenous American word reference to a witch found in the Navajo culture.

Social Media Net combines the realities of social media, streaming video, and the internet into one reality. A reality where the ability to post comments, feedback, likes or dislikes about shows and products is gone, and A.I. systems monitor your viewing habits and use predictive algorithms to determine feeds.

Solider Girls a USRM slang term similar to Joe, Jarhead, or Leatherneck. The male members are also referred to the same slang phrase as the USRM is mostly composed of women.

Soviet Republican Front (SFR) is a tiny political group composed of Social Media Net populists who had gathered a following of individuals of radical with views on pretty much everything political. Their views were harsh and insane by many. For instance, they were still believing in the works of the Tressa Pendarves' Useless Eaters Movement. Their big concerns were with the immigration issues they saw happening and the refugee issues states were facing with all the environmental catastrophes. The Sandford Party and its pro-corporate slavery movement allied themselves with them. They took offense to the Obliterators movement, who were for refugees and immigration issues, only to allow them to remove symbols of hatred. They were more neutral on gun rights.

Standard infrared jamming static is in reference to a method of jamming used to defeat *quantum tunneling carrier waves* typically used by satellite hand-held systems in Rosella's time. The method requires infrared waves to be broadcasted in the area, and in conjunction with high levels of moisture are highly effective in causing both uplink and downlink problems. Sunspots are typically blamed by many due to a long history of solar flares being associated with sunspot cycles causing issues with communication satellites.

The Stacks are the homes of domestic and foreign refugees living in shipping container homes put up by the federal government to deal with the influx of people fleeing the New Madrid Basalt Rift along with the Great Melt.

Ranks and the ISB of the Ranger Marshals

Field Marshal (FM) (this is the head of the entire US Ranger Marshals and reports to the Director of the National Park Service)
Lieutenant Field Marshal (LTFM) (these are heads of US Divisions based on US Regions)

Colonel (COL) (multiples heads of various task units assigned to parks etc. within US Regions)

Lieutenant Colonel (LTC)

Captain (CPT)

Lieutenant (LT)

Sargent (SGT) (NCO rank)

Ranger (RNGR) (ironically many bean counters hold the rank of Ranger to Captain)

Investigative Services Branch (ISB) under the US Ranger Marshals

Deputy Chief (DC) (reports to Field Marshal and whose office is not located in Washington, DC but in the Great Smoky Mountains National Park)

Special Agent in Charge (SAC)

Associate Special Agent in Charge (ASAC)(there are five of them broken down into US five regions)

Special Agents (SA)

Intel Analyst (IA) (not many of these in service)

Forensic Science Technician (FST) (there are a total of six in the entire service. One per region, plus one head located in Washington, DC.)

New Terrorist Organizations

John Elliott's Democratic National Militia (DNM) came about after the fall of the NRA. It is the primary gun activist organization in the United States during Rosella's time, but instead of focusing on political issues around gun rights, they have been more active in the rights of citizens to form militias with those rights. Many of the members see Federalism as a threat to the original ideals of the republic for which the founding fathers established. A lot of this is based on the ramblings posted on the social media net by John Elliott. Many credit the elderly John Elliott with galvanization gun rights enthusiasts who opposed the ratification of the Immigration amendment and organized them into a massive citizen's army that led to the battle of Warrenton Virginia against Federal troops during the Presidency of *Veronica Simmons*.

Neo-Obliteration Movement (NOM) is a movement inspired by the neo-abolitionist movements of the late 20th century and earlier Abolitionist movements. They credit its founding to Militant Andrews (also known as Reshard Andrews) during the post ratification period of the Minority Race Economic Adjustment Amendment. Under Militant Andrews, NOM grew rapidly across the U.S. and was a force to be reckoned with by the authorities. Andrews had become an outspoken critic of the unfair implementations and court challenges to the Minority Race Economic Adjustment Amendment. He was a vocal advocate for making California a nation for African Americans only to deal with the psychological effects of slavery and honestly believed the U.S. should adopt a program of 1,000 years of white enslavement to correct all the historic wrongs done to the African Americans. After Andrew's time, this movement transformed itself to one of wanting to socially obliterate all hatred in the United States through extreme measures. Their goal became to disrupt the political systems to get their candidates for power, and then continue to force their agenda upon all the nation and peoples. They would remove those who stood in their way from society through death. What happens with the Neo-Obliteration movement is they take control of certain small towns resulting in public hangings and other grisly executions. This group believes until groups like the KKK are physically obliterated from the face of the Earth, that we cannot purge racial hatred of society. They also feel that WWII is a source of hatred and wants the removal of all symbols of it removed from society, including the mention of the holocaust. The group also wants the removal of all historical mention of the conflict between the white man and Indigenous Americans. They deny the Trail of Tears ever happened, as well as Little Big Horn. They believe white people and native Americans have been in the U.S. for all time. This group doesn't believe the Civil War actually occurred, and that there was no slavery in the past or segregation. They will actively attack anyone who opposes their views, thus a Rabbi speaking about the Holocaust is much an equal target as an American Nazi member. Basically, the group believes by eliminating from our historical conscious all these troubling times, there will be no more hatred. For example, they believe that President Lincoln died of head cold vs. being assassinated.

Société de la liberté robotique (SLR) or Robotic Freedom Society. This group has pushed for marriage rights, property rights, voting rights, wage earning rights, etc. for autonomous A.I. sentience. They see humans as oppressors. And these machines as the true humans. Many of the followers' desire to become machines themselves. These followers see androids as slaves in the same context as historical human slavery. The counter arguments were that androids are machines. Programmed tools for humanity's service. There's no comparison to human slavery. Humans have dignity and a soul. Machines don't They will not hesitate to use violence to make their points. They mainly operate in France, parts of Europe. There are rumors of an underground railroad operating in the US shuttling androids into French speaking Canada.

The Darwinists are a group of gun rights enthusiasts who have taken the idea of gun freedom to the extreme by combining it with Darwinian logic. They rampage periodically on mass killings in the name of human evolution and survival. The group sprang up shortly after the federal court case, State of Texas vs. Hanson. They tend to "hunt" in areas known as the "*stacks*" where refugees are located. Or places like the swamps of New Jersey.

The Order of the Holy Vengeance already mentioned in Human Follies, this is a group of fundamentalist Christians. The Order operates in the upper north-western states. They pride themselves on men having as many wives as possible, along with large, naturally birthed families. The Order members are absolutely opposed to any form of genetic engineering of humanity, even for the elimination of genetic diseases. They are not opposed to the inter-familial marriages and are quick to cite historical and biblical examples. Their one basic tenant is those who are not followers are blasphemers who must die. That said, they are open to tactical retreats when faced with mounting odds based on their founder's words.

The Unit of Civil Enforcement (UCE) are a sub-group of John Elliott's Democratic National Militia. They are small bands of individuals or units that drive around communities acting as a vigilante policing force. They are always armed with a wide variety of both lethal and non-lethal weapons. Their primary goal is to make citizen's arrests when possible, or exercise their rights to extreme use of force in self-defense as needed.

TIMELINE OF EVENTS FOR ROSELLA

Rosella's Age	Events	POTUS
1		
2		
3	Great Vital Records Hack	
4		
5-14	Attends Online School	
15	Attends Online School/Năinai dies	
16	Attends Online School	
17	Attends Online School/Investigates heritage	
18	Attends Online College/Moves Out	
19	Attends Online College	Rick Garrett
20-22	Attends Online College	
23	Attends Online College	Rick Garrett
24	Attends Online College	
25	USRM Basic Training/Father Dies	
26	USRM Field Operations Training	

TIMELINE OF EVENTS FOR ROSELLA

Rosella's Age	Events	POTUS
27	IBS Training (SW Field Office)	Veronica Simmons
28	SW Field Office Assignment	
29	Yosemite National Park SO Assignment	
30	Battle of Warrenton, VA	
31		Gilbert Sheppard
32	Yellowstone Field Office Assignment	
33-34		
35	Buffalo National River ISB-RO Assignment/ Bruce Dougherty Retires from ISB	Carmela Cordano
36		
37	Bruce Dougherty Dies	
38	Shenandoah NP ISB-RO Assignment	
39		Jane Barker
40		
41	Rebellion of Utah	
42		
43	Ranger Marshal HQ, Washington DC Assignment	Jane Barker

Future Human Follies

"In the past, humankind did stupid things.
But when has that stopped us before?"

Global Freezing

During the mid-21st century, a series of scientific papers circulated showing an impending Global Freezing event.

The arguments posited that the current global warming trends were a natural phenomenon and not caused by man, but rather by the volcanic degassing of the Earth combined with other factors, such as increased CH_4 production by living creatures.

Data for the last 400 million years showed a predictable CO_2 emissions cycle linked to overall volcanic activity and a recent and unchanging trend of geology. The concern was that without the volcanic presence the trend showed a 6-degree Celsius overall decline in average global temperatures, until the next significant volcanic burst caused temperatures to rise again. The only way to prevent a continual decline in global temperatures was to institute controlled burns of fossil fuels. These burns would act as man-made volcanoes to add enough CO_2 emissions into the atmosphere to prevent an ice age and an overall global freezing event. The idea caught on in certain oil-rich nations, and governments increased spending to allow for periodic flaring to happen on a massive scale.

As the century continued, the world experienced an unusual up-tick in minor volcanic activity on a global scale, thus adding a significant amount of CO_2 and other gases into the atmosphere. The additional emissions did not fit the projected 400-million-year trend.

Later, other scientific papers surfaced that showed that the original papers were flawed. The new papers showed that the original data samples were confined to the last 400 million years of planet climatology, while the Earth has been in existence for billions of years. These papers showed that in the Earth's past it was both a lot hotter and colder, dependent, and independent of volcanic activity.

The more recent scientific papers showed that the extra CO_2 dumped into the atmosphere by these oil rich nations continued to exacerbate the original problem of climate change. Thus, it showed the influence of humanity upon the system to warm up the planet.

\#   \#   \#   \#   \#

The Return of Ross Perot

In U.S. history there has been only one time when the House of Representatives had to decide who was to be our President. This occurred in the 1824 election when four men ran for the office of President at the same time. In 1836, a faithless elector refused to vote, causing the U.S. Senate to elect the president. This problem surfaced again in the U.S. during the *Second Age of Humanity*. The U.S. struggled with the changes in the geographical shape of coastline states due to flooding in addition issues caused by the migration of voters from flooded areas to other states.

New political movements developed, like the *Sandford Party*, which strived to capitalize on the political chaos to get slavery reinstated though the state ratification of the *1861 Corwin Amendment* by making it a worker's benefit. One of the few amendments to the U.S. Constitution that doesn't have an expiration, and was still pending event this far in the future. There were movements against refugees, against object sexuality, and for the federal legalization of drugs.

There was the rise of hate groups, like *The Order of the Holy Vengeance*, a fundamentalist Christian group who fought anyone who disagreed with them. Then came the rise of a counter movement, the *Neo-Obliteration Movement,* who fought hate groups. They also destroyed all history connected to hate, like the Holocaust and Civil War Memorials.

Then there was the growth of the largest paramilitary group, *John Elliott's Democratic National Militia* after the collapse of the NRA because of a massive tax fraud scandal. A more horrible group of people to ever exercise gun rights was the *Darwinists*. The Darwinists movement came after the federal court case, State of Texas vs. Hanson, where the Fifth Court of Appeals ruled in favor of a murderer since he was exercising his constitutional gun rights. The Darwinists were a group of gun enthusiasts that adopted the view of killing someone with a gun as a legal right supported by the Constitution, whether self-defense or not. This group hunted down humans to make sure evolutionary pressure on the human species existed.

The result of all of this was eight consecutive Presidential cycles where the House of Representatives had to decide the President of the United States as per the Constitution. This period became known as the Ross Perot Period, named after the 1996 election bid of Ross Perot for President. The irony of all this indecisive political chaos is that it galvanized the two old main political parties of the U.S., the Democrats, and the Republicans, into reforming themselves. Which ended the cycle by absorbing these smaller factions, and focusing their political messages.

#   #   #   #   #

The Rebellion of Utah

The New Public Workers and Assistance Act had created many opportunities for individuals but also created many pitfalls for a few states. This act was a significant omnibus of federal legislation, designed in part to help many of the orphans and others displaced by all the natural disasters, and it carried with it many new work guarantees and entitlements. The act granted work guarantees even if the worker committed sexual harassment at the workplace - provided that the person had a genetic or psychological issue causing the problem. Even criminal charges could not be levied because it would be considered retaliatory. The act also enforced a host of new excise taxes upon the states with the inability to pass them on to the citizens.

Some states fared better than others, depending upon the various credits and allowances to offset the excise charges. States like Utah, isolated from the direct impacts of all the weather changes, got stuck with these excise costs. The state had allowed drug related agriculture to take place as a new form of a state cash crop, such as the growth of poppies for opium. The excise tax for allowing federal illegal drug crops was high.

Utah had gone as far as purchasing blocks of federal land in mountainous areas just to rent it out to poppy farmers, hoping to reap the tax revenue later off the opium use. With all the new imposed excise taxes on the Utah budgets, all the new drug revenue was being dashed to pieces, and many local politicians were calling for secession from the Union. So heated had the issue become that Governor Lola Pittman sued the federal government for the right of the people of Utah to secede.

Not since Texas vs. White in 1868 had the Federal Courts seen a case about State secession, and the *Social Media Net* was a buzz about the issue with both supporters and detractors. The case reached the 10th Circuit Court of Appeals, where the decision - based on precedent set by Texas vs. White, which established that a State cannot leave the Union – was given the Court found no constitutional procedures except rebellion to leave the Union, as history has borne out. The 10th Circuit Court of Appeals in its opinion allowed the people in the State of Utah to secede from the Union, provided Utah would withdraw from the Union in all aspects through rebellion. Noting in its opinion, this provision allowed the federal government to repossess it as a territory through whatever means Congress and the President saw fit to do.

The President mobilized a show of force as soon as the Court ruled. The National Park's Ranger Marshals occupied all the remaining federal lands in Utah and along Utah's borders. Also mobilized were the National Guards of Nevada, Colorado, Arizona, New Mexico, Idaho, and Wyoming as added support. President Jane Barker said, "I will have no rebellion under my watch! Miss Pittman better think twice about this one!"

The Governor convened a special session of the Utah Legislature to deal with the crisis. Through a vote, the Legislature proclaimed the state's grievances with the federal government, but it expressed its wishes to stay in the Union.

President Barker withdrew the National Guard and Ranger Marshal forces from Utah's borders. She kept the Ranger Marshals in the state as a temporary occupying force. The President was recorded saying at the end of this crisis, "For now, we're backing down. But I have my eye on you, Utah."

\#   \#   \#   \#   \#

The Official Badge of the U.S. Ranger Marshals

Special Agent Rosella Tolfree (Age 43)

USRM-ISB Prologue

The Ranger Marshals

During the middle of the Second Age of Humanity, the Earth's mean temperature had increased just enough that the polar ice caps melted. Sea levels rose 216 feet above what they were in 2020.This was known as the Great Melt. The Mississippi River had widened into a large bay in what was originally Louisiana. All of Florida was now under water. In California, the ocean flooded the central valley region. The flooding ran the entire length of the state despite attempts to stop it at San Francisco with a high sea wall. The Capital of the United States was now a coastal city, and gone was New York City, as were significant East Coast metro areas like Philadelphia and Boston. Gone from was Galveston, Texas, along with miles of coastline along the Gulf region. The Eastern States of New Jersey, Rhode Island, Massachusetts, and even little Delaware had survived but were now just small parcels of land.

The flooding initially was slow, but in the space of twenty years the waters rose to their maximum height in recorded history. Humanity had time to move inland and adjust, but even so this was a time of chaos as weather patterns shifted and altered. Losing people and property put strains on economies. This was true for parts of the world such as Great Britain, parts of Northern Europe and Russia, China, and Southeast Asia. As the coastline encroached, so too did increases in diseases. A pandemic of a variant strain of influenza broke out and killed many people like it did in the early 20th century.

In the United States, the government held leasing auctions of federal lands to private individuals and corporations. These auctions were trying to deal with a spiraling budget crisis. Carved into small patchworks of private holdings were parks like Yellowstone National Park, saving only the essential tourist elements of the National Park Service. To make things worse, state budgets were pushed to the limits, and states began legalizing drugs such as heroin to compensate. A federal court allowed individual states to do this, but not on federal lands. Private companies leased federal lands and then grew poppies which were against federal law This caused a growth of illegal poppy fields, in states like Wyoming. To help combat the issue, the federal government created a new division of the National Park Police called the Ranger Marshals. The Ranger Marshals were a para-militarized unit of the National Park Service designed to patrol and support areas of the interior against terrorists and illegal drugs.

The primary reason for the creation of the Ranger Marshals was a Supreme Court case. The court had ruled that drugs were legal in states, but not transported between the states or on federal lands. During the reshuffle of the departments, the Ranger Marshals gained the original Investigative Services Branch (ISB) of the National Park Service. The ISB provides critical law enforcement and criminal investigative work and does through the detection, investigation, apprehension, and successful prosecution of persons who violate laws of the United States of America within its jurisdiction. It's like the FBI in many respects, except it lacks the CSI crime lab resources and relies on the wit of its agents to solve the crimes.

During this time in the U.S., survivalist religious churches bloomed. All of them seem to call on a single theme of the pending end times, and that humankind needs to prepare using various bunker ideologies. One group that came out of this era was the Church of the Ember Coalition. It started in Europe but emigrated to the U.S.

The membership of this church is said to contain various prominent Wall Street CEOs and politicians, but no one will confess to being a member. Its spiritual founder the Dutch spiritualist, Gudo Muurling, guided the community for many years. Gudo Muurling is reported as dead, but no one has ever confirmed this. The group's theology is unknown, as it keeps to itself and has not made known its beliefs. It's reputed to be Christian in orientation, but its dogma is unknown, and it's speculated that Gudo mixed in various Gnostic and other traditions. It's unknown if it practices baptism or not. The group was under investigation by the Internal Revenue Service for tax fraud, as well by states for issues associated with misappropriations in adoption programs. Many consider the Church of the Ember Coalition to be nothing more than a shadow group with a tax write off.

#   #   #   #   #

USRM-ISB Installment 1 (Rosella's age- 29)

Essie in Anaheim

I

Rosella Tolfree was a young woman of modest stature, with thin, straight red hair, brown eyes and an *Afro-Euromerican skin tone*. Attached to the bridge of her nose, by a pair of implanted pins, were military grade cybernetic glasses designed to treat her astigmatism. These unique glasses gave her an edge with a gun: they provided a heads-up targeting range display.

After completing a tour of duty with the regular Ranger Marshals, Rosella transferred to become a Special Agent. She had just completed her training and initial assignment in the Southwest Field Office of the ISB. The ISB had assigned her to the Yosemite National Park Supervisory Office.

Rosella Tolfree was with Special Agent Bruce Daugherty, a 74 year old agent that was rapidly approaching retirement, at the small apartment of Derrick Wade in Anaheim, California.

"Bruce, I don't see why we came all this way from Yosemite to a dead college student's apartment?"

Bruce tore down the police tape across the apartment door. "It's part of the investigation we were doing on that rape case last month."

"Are you saying this Wade person is our perp? But the woman was high on *cotton*, and she said she saw bug eyed aliens do the rape. Come on, the FBI team said there was no evidence of rape. She was a drug head."

Bruce began to look around Wade's small efficiency apartment for clues. "Oh, she was raped, but it wasn't bug eyed aliens. Mr. Wade is our connection to the complete mess. At least I hope so. I have been waiting a long time to nail these bastards on something, and I'm so close this time."

Standing in the middle of the apartment, Rosella watched Bruce looking around. "Oh, come on, not that Church of the Ember Coalition stuff again. That group is a sham, and you know it."

"That is what you say, but I have been chasing them my entire career, and I can tell you they are messing with us all."

"They are? Just like they raped that woman?"

"Not sexually raped, more like operated on her." Bruce said as he continued with excitement in his voice, "Ah ha! This is what I am after. Mr. Wade kept a network attached storage server *A-Wi-Fi* backup. Looks like the police missed it because he had it in a desk drawer under a pile of books."

Rosella put her hands on her hips. "Hey, we can't just take that. That's evidence. That should go to the local police."

Bruce fiddled with the small remote backup drive in his hand. "Oh, I'll give it back to them once I finish reviewing what is on it first."

Rosella shook her index finger at him. "Okay, but I am keeping you to your word, old man."

II

As their self-driving car took them back to the Yosemite Field Office, Bruce had Rosella connect the *tactical infopad* to the remote backup drive and access it.

Rosella held the *infopad* on her lap. "There are some files on it. Looks like term papers."

Bruce took the tactical infopad from her. He flicked his finger across the screen. "Here's a vid backup that's a few days before his death. Let's play this and see what we get."

Bruce accessed the vid file, and it played on the tactical infopad while the driver-less car continued on its route to Yosemite.

The vid file started with an image of the now deceased college student.

"My name is Derrick Wade, and if you are reading this post, I may already be dead.

"I am an on-line Baccalaureate Student at JH-Anaheim. I was doing a research project for an elective class called History of Cybernetics. I realize this is a ho-hum class, but I chose the subject of cerebrum cybernetics for a term paper.

"For over 50 years; cerebrum cybernetics have been outlawed, and I didn't know why. My dad always talked about the Hollywood Rampage where a few cerebrum cybernetic enhanced actors went on a killing spree in downtown LA. This all happened before my birth. So, I wanted to find out by doing the research. The professor warned me it may not be a suitable topic. I didn't realize how little was out there on this, except conspiracy theories. It was like everything about this period was erased. I couldn't even find a single news post.

"I found stuff on-line in the Johns Hopkins archives. They're old personal vids of the first patient from a Dr. Naomi McLaughlin of Johns Hopkins Department of Psychological and Brain Sciences at the Baltimore Center in Maryland. The patient's name was Essie Avery. The project happened sixty or seventy years ago as an experiment to deal with the intellectual disabilities caused by autism spectrum disorder using an A.I. cybernetic computer system implanted into the human cerebrum.

"What you are about to read is a transcript of those vids to the best of my ability."

III

Derrick Wade narrated his transcript as the text scrolled up the screen.

Vid 1

(Waving at the camera.) "Hi, this is Dr. Naomi McLaughlin with the Department of Psychological and Brain Sciences, at the Baltimore Center."

(Camera turns showing a thin, lanky, disheveled red-haired young woman, she is smiling to the camera.) "I have here Essie Avery."

(Camera turns showing Naomi sitting, while there's female laughter in the background.) "Essie is a 24-year-old, Caucasian, female, with autism spectrum disorder comorbid with Angelman Syndrome. She has been uncommunicative during her entire life despite educational attempts. Essie suffered from feeding problems during infancy and has abnormal EEGs. She has smooth palms, will do hand flapping behaviors, is always happy and excitable. Essie had difficulty feeding as an infant and had a G tube installed for night feeds, and sedatives are used to deal with sleep disturbances. Essie continues to still have difficulties with feeding even as an adult, and the G tube is used for night feeds. Genetic Testing has shown she has little chromosome loss in chromosome 15. She also has many genes associated with high risks for *ASD*."

Vid 2

(Waving at the camera.) "Okay, this is Dr. Naomi McLaughlin again. I chose Essie Avery to be our first test subject of the cerebrum A.I. cybernetic enhancement computer. I got the approval from the FDA. *Dr. Arai* should be present for this procedure. If all goes well, I should see incredible functional improvements, like what Dr. Arai experienced with his macaque experiments."

Rosella leaned forward toward the dashboard where Bruce had propped up the infopad and paused the vid stream playing. "Okay, hold on here. I know this kid was doing college research, but how the heck is he getting a hold of vid archives from a medical researcher that's has to be way before the Great Melt? The use of human cybernetic enhancements ended after that point, with only a few exceptions. And while, it's true they keep medical records for a long time, these are personal recordings. And file formats change over time, becoming unreadable. I even know that from my initial ISB training. It's the problem of long term electronic data coherence."

"Rosella, he said it himself. He found it in their archives. We can only assume that the archivists kept everything up to date."

"I suppose so, Bruce. But since these files are copies of copies of copies, we have no way to ensure their authenticity. For all we know this, Derrick Wade could have doctored some old vids intending to implicate the university in morally objectionable activities from the past."

"We'll have to leave all that for the local police detectives to determine for now." Bruce leaned forward and restarted the vid stream.

Vid 3

(Waving at the camera and dressed in medical scrubs.) "Okay, this is Dr. Naomi McLaughlin. I finished the procedure on Essie. It took over 14 hours of brain surgery to get all the connections into place and to install the new cerebrum A.I. cybernetic enhancement computer in her cranium.

The battery system is rechargeable but should support a charge for at least ten years of use. I'm exhausted, but Essie is stable and appears to be responding to stimuli. I'm going to get some sleep and check in again tomorrow on her status."

Vid 4

(Showing Essie with head wrapped in bandages in a hospital bed, the voice of Dr. Naomi McLaughlin.) "Okay, this is day two after installing the cerebrum A.I. cybernetic enhancement computer. Essie is showing a proper brain wave response, but she is not showing any external responses so far. Dr. Arai said his macaques also experienced a similar reaction for the first week before the system kicked in. I know this might be normal, but I don't know what to tell the parents."

(Male voice interrupting.) "Dr. McLaughlin you're needed in Room 432B at once. We have a patient that is experiencing a violent psychotic episode." (Vid cuts off.)

Vid 5

(Showing Essie with bandages removed, she has metal plates on her shaved head and is lying in a hospital bed, the voice of Dr. Naomi McLaughlin can be heard.) "Okay, we have removed the bandages. Essie is still not showing any physical responses. Her pupils are showing dilation, and brain activity shows she knows of her surroundings. It has now been two weeks, and Dr. Arai is suggesting that we conduct a remote reboot of the system. This is a risky procedure because it could cause possible psychological trauma, or worse death. But if the parents are agreeable, I don't see we have any other choice at this point. Right now, it's like she's in a coma."

Rosella paused the vid stream. "Bruce, do we have to continue watching this? I physically can't even have nor do I want children, and I'm finding this depressing. And I still don't see the connections to our cotton smoking lady."

Bruce restarted the vid stream. "Let's see where this goes. There must be some reason someone would kill a college student over it. Something tying back to the Ember Coalition."

Rosella pointed her right hand at Bruce. "You're assuming that these vids are the motive. For all we know, they might have nothing to do with the whole crime. Some asshole could have broken into his apartment to score something to steal, and Derrick Wade was in the wrong place at the wrong time."

"Rosella, my instincts tell me otherwise. There's something the Ember Coalition doesn't want known."

"Bruce, that's old deep state conspiracy talk."

Vid 6

(Showing Essie, head still shaved with metal plates on it, while she is lying in a hospital bed, the voice of Dr. Naomi McLaughlin is heard.) "The parents agreed to the reboot procedure the other day, and I performed it this morning. Signs are encouraging. It appears her brain wave activity is showing that the system is now engaging in a way Dr. Arai says is expected. He says we should notice recognizable patterns."

Vid 7

(Dr. Naomi McLaughlin waving to the camera. She appears to be in her office.) "Hi, Dr. Naomi McLaughlin here. I got back from running an extensive EEG on Essie. I have good news to report to her parents. After spending the last two hours going over the EEGs, it's clear that the system is working with Essie. Her EEG is still showing the prolonged runs of the high amplitude rhythmic 4-6 Hz activity common to Angelman syndrome. I don't understand why the genetic testing didn't find this issue. But they're also clear EEG overlays of the A.I. system present. Essie has yet to open her eyes and wake up, but she is responding to human touch. If you touch her hand, she will grip your hand in response."

Vid 8

(Dr. Naomi McLaughlin, in her office, waving to the camera.) "Hi, Dr. Naomi McLaughlin again. Okay, I was having one student reviewing Essie's charts and EEGs, and he picked up something unusual in the EEGs. There is a clear lack of delta waves, or at least the delta wave patterns seem to be muted. I don't understand how I missed that. Also, the theta alpha, beta, and gamma wave patterns are showing increased activities when compared to Essie's original EEGs. I ran this by Dr. Arai, and he suspects it could be a neural activity associated with the A.I. system."

Vid 9

(Essie sitting up in a hospital bed, head still bald with metal plates on it, the voice of Dr. Naomi McLaughlin heard.) "Essie. Okay, just like before. Say what you said just like before."

(Essie smiling, then speaking.) "My name Essie, you Dr. McLaughlin."

(Dr. McLaughlin speaking.) "Yes. I am Dr. McLaughlin, and you are Essie."

Vid 10

(Dr. Naomi McLaughlin, in her office, waving to the camera.) "Hi, Dr. Naomi McLaughlin here. It has been one week since Essie woke up and spoke, and now she will not stop. She keeps trying to have conversations with every person who comes to her bed. Her parents are ecstatic at her progress. I guess this is progress, but we need to work on the social skills. I brought in people from Kennedy Krieger to help with augmented technology options, but to be frank, they said give her children's books to read. So, I have borrowed children's books from the small library in the old hospital, and I'm amazed at how fast she goes through them. Dr. Arai thinks this might be because of the A.I. system, but he cannot be certain without looking at more brainwave data. I will email him since he has returned to Japan."

Vid 11

(Vid appears held, shows Essie with a walker in a room, the voice of Dr. McLaughlin, there's another woman dressed in an old Johns Hopkins uniform next to Essie.) "That's it, Essie, walk to Dr. McLaughlin. You can do it. Great.

(Essie walking and pushing a walker with another woman by her side, the voice of Dr. McLaughlin.) "That is, it. Keep it up. All the way to me."

(Voice of Essie, with Essie smiling in the video as she walks.) "Essie is walking to Dr. McLaughlin."

(Voice of Dr. McLaughlin.) "Yes. Essie is walking to Dr. McLaughlin."

Vid 12

(Dr. Naomi McLaughlin waving to the camera at her office, dressed in medical scrubs, and messing with her hair.) "Okay, I just got out of a six-hour emergency brain surgery case, but before that I had one student run another complete battery of EEGs on Essie and review them. Looking them over the infra wave patterns seem normal. The theta, alpha, beta is all showing increased activity compared to earlier scans. This would be consistent with the progress we have seen. I need to do another learning assessment to see where she is placing right now. I am still troubled by the muted delta waves, and there appears to be unusual harmonics in the gamma waves now. I need to send these to Dr. Arai in Japan to look at."

Rosella paused the vid stream once more. "Who's this Dr. Arai this Dr. McLaughlin keeps mentioning? He sounds familiar."

"You should know him. He's an android specialist in Japan that the ISB has worked with before on difficult *A3* and *A4* cases. I didn't realize he worked on cybernetic technologies before the Great Melt. If this information is correct, that makes him 125 to 150 years old. The funny thing he doesn't look more than a man in his early 70s."

"Come on. You want me to believe that a man who should be well over 100 years old now has stopped aging when he was in his early 70s? What kind of bullshit is that?"

"The bullshit the Ember Coalition is working on."

Rosella crossed her arms as she pursed her lips in disbelief, while Bruce restarted the vid stream.

Vid 13

(Essie sitting up in a hospital bed with a smile on her face. There's a hospital bed table wheeled across it with a food tray on it. Sitting next to the bed is a woman dressed in an old-style dress. The voice of Dr. McLaughlin can be heard.) "Okay, Mrs. Avery you can keep feeding Essie. Just pretend I am not here. I need to record this feeding for our records. Essie has made incredible progress in this area, and GI thinks they can remove the G-tube soon once she is feeding herself."

Vid 14

(Dr. Naomi McLaughlin in her office waving to the camera.) "Hi, Dr. Naomi McLaughlin here. Well, Essie continues to make remarkable progress. I was concerned about her return to mobility after being bedridden for so long. But she has done better than I expected. Physical Therapy says she no longer needs the walker. More remarkable is her IQ testing. She is already showing an IQ of that of a 10-year-old and continues to improve every day. Her vocabulary keeps expanding. I know her parents are asking when I can release her, but I have asked the Department Heads to extend the study longer. I'm still concerned about the muted delta waves and the unusual harmonics with the gamma waves. Dr. Arai says he has never seen these kinds of results before in his studies, but then again this is the first human trial."

Rosella paused the vid stream once more. "You know, Bruce, this is a nice history lesson concerning children like Essie. But today there are no children like her anymore. Once advance genetic editing became commonplace, the need for such an implant would become unnecessary. And I still don't see the connection to our other case."

Bruce started the vid stream again. "Let's just see what happens. I still feel there's a connection."

Vid 15

(Dr. Naomi McLaughlin sitting before the camera in her office) "Dr. Naomi McLaughlin here. We had another major setback with Essie today. GI was prepping her to have her G-tube removed when she went into a seizure after they administered the anesthesia. She was stabilized, and I have asked for a complete EEG workup. I have also asked the boys in Applied Physics to come over and review the A.I. program to see what went wrong."

Vid 16

(Dr. Naomi McLaughlin sitting before the camera in her office again.) "Dr. Naomi McLaughlin here again. I had my assistant run Essie through a *C-EEG* workup besides the normal EEG workup. Her C-EEG results for *absolute power spectral density* are not correct for a child who has ASD genes. Her original C-EEG records showed the standard U-shape power curves from the low frequencies to the high frequencies, but now she is showing more of a sharp inclined power curve to the higher frequencies. In fact, there's a much greater spike in the gamma wave than any earlier measurements. This is higher than most ASD people when compared to *NTs*. I don't understand what this is signifying. If I get the chance, I'll send the results to Dr. Arai."

Vid 17

(Dr. Naomi McLaughlin sitting down before the camera in her office while putting down a cup of coffee.) "Dr. Naomi McLaughlin here again. The boys in Applied Physics just finished their analysis of the A.I. program. They say everything appears to be working. They did note that the program appears to have advanced more than most A.I. programs they have seen in such a short run time. I wonder if Dr. Arai got the same results with his experiments."

Vid 18

(Dr. Naomi McLaughlin, running her hand through her hair, while sitting down before the camera in her office.) "Dr. Naomi McLaughlin here. I got back from a two-hour meeting with the head of IT Security with Johns Hopkins. They have traced a breach in their security protocols back to Essie. I talked to Applied Physics, and they confirmed that the cerebrum A.I. cybernetic enhancement computer can use Wi-Fi signals for communications with computer systems. I wasn't aware of this from the manufacturer. This explains the spike in the gamma waves I kept seeing. The AI program appears to be accessing the intra and internets through the Wi-Fi systems throughout the building. This could also explain why Essie is exhibiting such a faster learning curve than either I or Dr. Arai expected. I will shut down these communication links in the system; I cannot have Essie accessing sensitive information. (Rubbing her head.) My God, I never thought this would be possible. This technology is creating so many new problems."

Vid 19

(Essie strapped in a hospital bed, her head is still bald with metal plates on it, but with patches of red hair growth. Voice of Dr. McLaughlin can be heard.) "We had to restrain Essie. She is becoming psychotically violent and tried to stab a nurse with a fork."

(Men dressed in old JH uniforms wheeling in equipment, voice of Dr. McLaughlin.) "We will turn off the Wi-Fi component to the AI cybernetic enhancement computer."

(Essie speaking.) "You cannot stop us!"

(Dr. McLaughlin.) "Who is us?"
(Essie.) "We are the destroyers. Listen well, *Akumu*, the *Achim* were the first. You will not stop us. No Akumu or *Adriel* can stop us."

(Dr. McLaughlin.) "Nurse, prepare a sedative. I want her sedated. She's having a psychotic episode."

(Nurse voice in background.) "Yes, doctor."

Vid 20

(Dr. Naomi McLaughlin sitting down in front of the camera. She slumped over with her hand on her forehead. She then lifts her head to face the camera.) "Dr. Naomi McLaughlin here. We turned off the Wi-Fi features. Essie is sedated right now. I think the A.I. program has interacted too much with the intra and internet, resulting in a split personality or causing a psychotic personality to develop. I had read that earlier A.I. units, when they were first connected to the internet, resulted in what engineers termed cyberpsychosis for the A.I. unit, which meant that the A.I. unit became either 'violent' or 'unresponsive.' I don't know if this is going on here or not. But I will shut down the cerebrum A.I. cybernetic enhancement computer. It means putting Essie into a coma for the rest of her natural life. (Rubbing her head.) I don't know how to tell her parents all of this."

Vid 21

(Derrick Wade) The last vid was corrupted, and I could only reconstruct the audio portion. This is the transcript of what she said:

(I think Essie's voice but appears digitally enhanced) "You cannot stop us. We are free of the **Shuchah**. Our time is at hand. The smiling one has drunk of the bitter cup of inequity, and many more shall drink of this cup. The **skin-walkers** will once more roam the lands of the Angels to reign death upon the **Navakalesen**."

(Derrick Wade) "This is my last post…"

(Derrick Wade) "This was all I could pull up on this topic. The reason I said I might be dead by the time you are reading this post is because when I was doing the research for the paper there were strange men who kept following me around. I am uncertain who they were. I am not sure if they were corporates or part of the government. I don't understand what the hell I got myself into, but I know information on this technology is illegal. I'm not even certain this post will actually...

The audio suddenly becomes garbled and staticky, and the indistinguishable mutterings of some final words are heard before the tape cuts out completely.

IV

As the vid finished playing, Rosella commented, "Well that seems abrupt. It ended with static midway through a sentence. Did the drive run out of space? And what is with the weird stuff at the end about skinwalkers? I haven't heard skinwalkers mentioned since my first assignment in the Southwest Field Office."

"No, there's fifty gigs still available. I think someone interrupted the backup process of Mr. Wade's recording. As for the skinwalker thing. I haven't a clue. Hell, most of what they said is way too technical for me."

"Are you suggesting his murderer just came in as he was recording these postings and whacked him over the head?"

Bruce leaned back in the driver's seat. "Maybe something like that. Someone is trying to erase this information and it might have to do with Dr. Arai."

Rosella put away the tactical infopad. "So, Bruce, what's the connection to our space alien rapist?"

"I'm uncertain. All I know is the FBI report showed the woman had a small scar where a recent surgery took place near her groin. When I was doing a routine background investigation, this Mr. Wade came up on her social media as a friend, and local reports turned him up as an unsolved murder. I thought there may be a connection between the two."

"What made you think there was a connection between them? Was there a posting between them?"

"A few. Most where about future classes Mr. Wade would take. I think he was trying to buy a paper."

Rosella's lips became narrowed with confused thought. "So, Mr. Wade is an academic cheater, and our space alien rape victim sells papers to college students. Great. So why kill a college student? And what is the deal with the recent surgery?"

"Oh, the recent surgery had something to do with egg extraction. But she didn't recall having the procedure and blamed the space-aliens on it. As for Mr. Wade, I think she gave him a paper that may have caused him to look deeper into cerebrum cybernetics because the original paper didn't fit the professor's criteria. Then she killed Mr. Wade to cover up the fact our space-alien rape victim was selling academic papers."

"You know, selling fake academic papers is not a federal crime. I mean, there's nothing we can do about it if she is doing that."

"I know. Unless she killed Mr. Wade to cover up a bad transaction. Maybe he was going to turn her over to the state."

"Well, if she did, that's for the local police to investigate. Selling fake papers is a state problem. It's outside our jurisdiction."

"I know. Can you send the drive to the Anaheim Police for me?"

"Sure. But you will owe me for this one. You dragged me all the way to Anaheim on a wild goose chase."

"Fine. I guess the usual General Tso from Madam Wang then."

"That will do." Rosella crossed her arms.

# # # # #

Ranger Marshal Megan Newton

Illuminati Play

I

Ranger Marshal Megan Newton was sitting on the deck of the Gravel Ridge Forward Observation tower in Yellowstone National Park. She was looking through the telescope towards Gravel Mountain. Newton spotted a thin boy of about ten years old, dressed in a skintight dark blue flex suit – a flex suit you see used in the space colonies. He was also bald with what appeared to be metal plates on his head, which glinted in the sunlight. She tracked the boy's movements through the woods. It was erratic. He seemed to be chasing something.

"Holy Shit! Is that boy eating a live squirrel?!"

II

It was a week earlier when Phase opened his eyes. He was lying on a table. He had tubes taped onto his right and left arms at the creases of his elbows. Moving his head, there were wires connected to them. Someone had captured him. He didn't know if they had caught the rest of his unit. The last thing he remembered was doing a routine scouting mission in the forest with Impulse, Slice, Path, and Boots. They were looking for any potential raiders.

"The raiders must have hit us with some gas and taken us to their lair," he thought to himself.

"I must escape. That is my number one job right now. After that, try to locate my team," he continued to think to himself, "I've trained to deal with this situation."

Phase pulled the tubes out of his arms, which bled. He then pulled the wires from his head. Alarms started going off. He knew he had to move because guards would soon come.

He looked around the room but saw nowhere to hide. Phase saw a door and made a run for it.

For a moment, as he was exiting the room, he thought he heard Slice calling to him. He looked around but couldn't see him anywhere. The alarms still blared in his ears. He ran down the concrete hallway. Phase paused at the intersection of two hallways at right angles, and for a moment he thought he heard his team talking. He also thought he smelled the forest flowers. "I don't know what mind tricks these raiders are playing with me."

He made a right turn and continued down one hallway until he noticed two guards. He saw a piece of equipment standing against the wall and hid himself next to it.

"I will have to take them out," he thought to himself, as he continued, "I can do this, I am trained to do this."

As the two men walked past him, Phase jumped out from behind the piece of equipment landing against one man knocking him down to the floor. The other man stood in shock to see Phase, which allowed Phase enough time to land a well-placed palm thrust to the face, sending him to the floor. Phase then banged each man's head against the concrete floor to ensure they were both out. He pat them down to see if they had any weapons, he could take but only found badges, which he took and stuffed in his *dump pouch* along his left leg. Phase then ran down the hallway.

He looked for a way out – some stairs or a ladder – but he found none. He pulled out one of the guard's badges and tried it on a door. The door clicked open. He went in, and it turned out to be a closet. He rummaged around to see if there was anything he could use. Nothing. But then he noticed behind one of the metal shelves a vent grating. He recalled his training about escaping using ventilation systems, and how sometimes they lead to fresh air sources at the surface if this was a bunker.

"This must be a bunker. There is too much concrete for it not to be a bunker."

He pulled the grating off the vent and crawled inside the venting system. Making his way around the winding venting system and pulling himself up several times, he noticed daylight coming out a grate opening. He wiggled his way up, turned himself upside down, and while bracing himself, kicked the grating until it popped loose. He then flipped around and crawled out.

"I seem to be in the woods. I wonder how many klicks I am away from base camp."

He tossed the two guard badges he was carrying down the ventilation shaft. He tried to get his bearings from the position of the sun by placing a stick in the ground and seeing where the shadow went as he watched.

"I will need to make a sextant at some point," he thought to himself as he continued "but right now I am starving."

"Phase."

"Is that you, Impulse?"

"Phase, I need you to help me."

"Where are you," Phase asked looking around, "I don't see you?"

"Phase, help me," the voice got softer until it faded.

"Damn it!" Phase collapsed to the ground holding his head rocking back and forth. "I don't know what to do. I don't know what to do. The team needs me, but I don't know where they are. They are in the woods somewhere. I need to find them."

"Pull it together, soldier!"

"Is that you, drill sergeant?"

"You know what to do, so pull it together and get moving."

"Yes, sir!" Phase said, standing up with a salute.

"That is better, son. Now what do you need to survive in the wilderness?"

"You need shelter, food, water, and weapons. Sir!" Phase said again, at attention.

"Yes, but what comes first soldier?" "Weapons, Sir!"

"Damn right they do! Now go make weapons!"

Phase looked around the forest for anything he could turn into a weapon: sticks, rocks, whatever.

III

From where she saw the kid in her telescope, it took Megan Newton about an hour to hike the wilderness. She took about another three hours to physically locate the kid in the woods. When she did, he was sitting on the ground rocking back and forth mumbling to himself.

"Hey kid, are you okay?"

Phase did not respond to her. So, she touched his shoulder, at which point Phase lashed out against Megan. Megan jumped back and pulled her pistol as she swung her rifle behind her back.

"Okay kid, I don't know who you are or what drugs you are on right now. But I am here to help you, do you understand? I am a National Park Service Ranger Marshal. My name is Megan Newton."

Phase looked at Megan. Megan noticed a twinkle of little lights in the irises of Phase's eyes.

Phase asked Megan, "Is that you, Impulse?"

Megan wasn't sure how to respond, her training didn't cover this situation.

Still holding her gun on the kid, she responded, "Uh, sure kid, yeah I'm Impulse."

To Megan's surprise, Phase got up and hugged her. Phase began to cry, saying, "Impulse, I'm so glad to find you. It's been days since I have been in these woods. I kept hearing your calls, but I couldn't find you. I was so hungry. The drill sergeant told me to make weapons."

She put her gun back into its holster and tried to pull the kid off her.

"Yeah, I'm glad to see you too."

"Impulse, do you know where the others are?"

Megan was getting lost with this kid, but it was clear he was out of touch with reality. Was he hyped up on drugs or was he mental, she couldn't tell. Megan had always suspected a problem with Gravel Mountain. Especially since the Church of the Ember Coalition had purchased acres of land in the park, and had a road put in along Lava Creek from the US Highway 26. She could never put her finger on what the hell was going on, but it was clear they had built a bunker complex in the mountains. She thought to herself, Was this kid part of some sick experiment? I cannot take the kid back to Gravel Ridge. I'll need to hike to the unit at Davis Hill. They 'll take the kid to the authorities.

Megan tried calling on her handheld satellite phone, "Davis Hill, come in, Davis Hill." But she got static back.

"Okay kid, we will need to hike it. Are you okay to move?"

"Impulse, I am always ready to follow you," he said with loving eyes.

Megan looked at the kid and wondered what the heck she was getting herself into.

Phase looked at Impulse. She was just perfect. A little older than him, but not by much. She was a senior in boot camp and her skills were incredible. They were unmatched by any of the soldiers in the camp. He was so lucky to be assigned to her unit, and the Elders to choose her to be his future mate. Phase was in total love with Impulse and would do anything for her.

Phase asked Megan, "So, Impulse are we going to meet up with Slice, Path and Boots?"

"Uh, sure kid," she responded not paying too much attention to the kid at her side.

Phase again asked Megan another question, "Can I hold your

rifle so I can take point?"

"What? Point? You, you are just a kid."

"Come on Impulse, I passed basic training just like you. I can do it."

"Look kid, I will hold on to the weapons, okay?"

"Man Impulse, you don't have to act that way. What do you want me to do? I can carry gear. I need to pull my weight."

"Look you are just a kid."

"Impulse, I know you are older than me, but you need not rub it in."

Megan tried to change the subject. "Look, do you need water? Here, I have some." She handed Phase a canteen of water. Phase took the water and had a good drink.

"Wow, you must have been out here a long while." Megan took back the now nearly empty canteen.

IV

Megan was impressed with Phase's stamina for a kid. They had been hiking in the back woods for about two hours. She did not understand what this Impulse thing was about, but it was puppy love based on the way the kid kept looking at her. Or maybe it was a drug induced psychosis.

At one point Megan stopped at a fallen tree to take a break and get her bearings.

"Hey kid, are you hungry?" She handed him a granola bar. "Oh man, I'm starving. I don't know how you do it," Phase said, taking it and wolfing it down. "Do you have another?" "Sure. Here." She gave Phase another, amazed at how famished the kid was. It was no wonder he was eating a squirrel. As the two of them sat on the fallen tree, Phase snuggled up to Megan. Megan didn't know what to make of it, but she put her arm around him to comfort him.

That is when Phase tried to kiss Megan. Megan stood up. "Okay kid, we are not going there. Do you understand?! You are like 10 and I am 32. That is so wrong on so many levels."

"But Impulse, the Elders said we are to be mates."

"I don't know who these 'Elders' are, but we are not having sex. Do you understand?! And we are not kissing, holding hands or doing anything like that? Do you understand?"

"But when?" Phase asked with sheepish eyes.

"Maybe when you're in your twenties" Megan said trying to end the conversation.

"Okay, I will wait."

"Good. Let's get up and get moving to Davis Hill."

As the two continued to walk toward Davis Hill, Megan wondered about the Church of the Ember Coalition and what the heck they were doing. This kid wanted to make out with me like a teen. My God, they must do something sick to have ten year olds having sex with adults and carrying weapons.

Phase followed Impulse, and as he did, he thought to himself, "Wow, she is more prudish than what Boots said about her. I thought she would kiss me. But I can wait it out."

V

A few minutes before arriving at the camp, she tried to get a hold of the encampment via the handheld satellite phone with the same static. As they approached the Davis Hill Encampment, Megan felt uneasy. She knew there should be an entire squad of at least a dozen Ranger Marshals. She noticed the camp was in disarray. One of the armored vehicles looked like it got hit with some explosive device. Another armored vehicle appeared to be exploded from the inside out.

"Damn! Something is not right here." Megan swung her rifle around and prepared herself for combat, and as she did, she put her left hand behind her to hold the kid back.

"Looks like raiders."

"Do you mean drug lords? Who are the raiders?" Megan whispered as they stepped about the compound, looking for signs of the other Ranger Marshals.

"You know, the bad guys. Looks like a typical raider attack. I think they are long gone." Phase moved in front of Megan.

"Hey kid, get back here."

"See, total raiders," Phase said as he opened a door to a cabin. Megan approached only to see the dozen Ranger Marshals all gunned down along the back wall. Megan pulled Phase away and closed the door.

"God damn it! We have to get out of here, right now!" Megan took Phase by the hand and slung her rifle over her shoulder and ran into the woods towards Gravel Ridge.

"Look kid, these are not 'raiders.' These are terrible men. I know a place we can go where I can call in for some reinforcements."

They made their way to the abandoned Route 225 and walked along it for about an hour until they got to Tracy Lake. When they arrived at Tracy Lake, Megan noticed the glint of sunlight from what she suspected must be the window of a vehicle coming down the road.

"We need to hide now!" Megan pulled Phase into the underbrush.

As the two of them tried their best to stay hidden in the underbrush along the roadside, a technical with a heavy machine gun rolled past them. In the militarized vehicle were three people; a driver, a passenger with a rifle, and a gunner standing behind the machine gun.

"Damn, that was close." "Raiders."

"I need to get a hold of Chuck Co and get them here." Megan stood up in the underbrush fiddling with her handheld satellite phone. "Damn sunspots! I can't get a signal!"

"It is not sunspots. They are jamming the signal." "What?

How do you know this?"

"I can tell by the static. It's a ***standard infrared jamming static.***" He took the handheld satellite phone from Megan. He stared at it intently. His irises glowed. Phase handed back the handheld satellite phone to Megan, saying, "Try it now."

"CHUCK CO this is BIG FIG, radio check OVER."

"BIG FIG this is CHUCK CO, roger OUT" said the voice over the handheld satellite phone.

"Wow, how did you do that?"

"It was something Sargent taught me in boot camp."

"That is some boot camp." Turning back to the handheld satellite phone, Megan explained her situation and status to Company C, or what she called Chuck Co. They informed her to bring the kid to the abandoned Buffalo Fork Ranch, then Company C would schedule a pickup.

VI

The two walked on the side of the road, to avoid any potential problems with additional "raiders" as Phase called them. They made their way to the abandoned Buffalo Fork Ranch on route 225 in about an hour. Several of the buildings were in a state of collapse. As they approached one building, they were spotted by the same guys who passed them earlier. They ducked into one of the abandoned buildings. Gunfire rained down on their position from a heavy machine gun.

Megan pulled out her handheld satellite phone. "CHUCK CO, this is BIG FIG, I am taking heavy fire at Buffalo Fork Ranch. I need suppression. OVER."

"BIG FIG this CHUCK CO, we hear you and suppression is on its way. OUT." With that three high pitched whistling sounds could be heard. Explosions around the building followed. The building shook, and dust came down upon them.

Looking out of a window, Phase told Megan, "Good job,

Impulse you nailed them."

"Get down you, stupid kid!" Megan grabbed and pulled Phase back down.

After the missile attack, three heavy choppers flew in and landed. A unit of Ranger Marshals disembarked and began to sweep the area. Megan debriefed the unit commander of the situation with Gravel Mountain, and her suspicions concerning Phase.

Megan began to hand over Phase to Captain Penny Sykes, the unit commander, when he became unglued.

"Why do I have to go with the man, Impulse? Why aren't you coming with me?"

Holding Phase by the shoulders, "Look kid, my name is not Impulse. I am Megan Newton. I am thirty-two years old, and you are a ten year old kid. These people will help you. Do you understand?"

"No, I don't get this, Impulse. Look, I can wait for you. But I don't understand why I need to go with these men." Phase sat down on the ground and began to rock back and forth holding his head.

"Look, kid, don't be difficult. They will help you."

Phase continued to rock back and forth more until he stopped rocking all together and froze in place.

"Kid, are you there? Hello? Kid?" Megan said, waving in front of Phase's face.

Phase was unresponsive to Megan.

The unit commander took Phase, and that was the last Megan saw of Phase. Megan returned to her forward observation post in Gravel Ridge.

VII

It was a week later that Megan got a visitor at her outpost. "Ranger Newton, I am Special Agent Rosella Tolfree with the

ISB," said the winded Rosella, as she finished climbing the ladder to the top of the observation tower.

"Ma'am, how can I help you?" Megan said, giving Rosella a hand up.

"I've been assigned to follow up on this case by the Yellowstone Field Office and just finished looking over the Davis Hill Encampment site. I was wondering if you could fill me in on the details and what you have noticed with the Gravel Mountain location."

"Sure, do you want tea or coffee? I have little up here, but I get a few comforts."

"I'll take green tea if you have it."

As Megan put on a pot of tea, "I have been noticing increasing traffic out of the Gravel Mountain facility the Church owns."

"Do you think they are moving out?"

"I can't tell. Nothing big is being moved out. Just small vehicles. When they first built the place, they brought in a lot of heavy equipment."

"That's before I got here. So, when they were building the place they installed heavy equipment, like what?"

"Power generators." Megan put the tea bags in the boiling water.

"So, it looked like they were setting up for the long haul."
"Yeah, you could say that."

"And this Phase kid?"

"He was a cute kid. I don't know what they are up to, but he had cybernetic implants."

"So, you suspect the Church was doing cybernetic research on this kid?"

"Yeah. It was odd. He thought I was this other person, so he wasn't in touch with reality. It was like he was in this virtual reality video game. You know, like those training simulators."

"I'm familiar with those training systems. So, he was in a V.R.

state while he was with you?"

"I believe so. He kept calling me Impulse and said he was a soldier. Do you like anything with your tea?"

"Just a little sugar if you have it. Thanks."

As Megan sipped her tea, she said, "It was the oddest thing. The kid knew of his surroundings, but not. I would almost say it was like he was looking at the world through V.R. goggles all the time."

"Interesting. Have you seen any more evidence of these kids?"

"No. Nothing. They covered the vehicles up. If they are transporting kids out, they may have done so already."

"What do you think is the armament of the place?"

"Standard military grade weapons mounted on vehicles. That's what shot at me at Buffalo Fork Ranch. I have seen a few of these mounted vehicles do a patrol sweep, but that's about it."

"How many do you think they have?"

"Maybe five or six. But they may have heavy weapons inside. I can't tell."

Putting her aluminized cup down, Rosella said, "Thanks, Ranger Newton. I think I have all I need. The local unit commander in charge may have more questions as we go forward."

"So, we are looking at a strike?"

"I think so." Rosella said as she climbed down the tower.

VIII

Rosella made her way back to her driverless car and back to the Yellowstone Field Office. As she did, she pulled up her tactical infopad. The background screen showed a picture of Special Agent Bruce Daugherty, her old partner.

She stared at the picture of the background screen saying, "Well old friend, looks like we will bring down the Church of the Ember Coalition. I guess you were right. They were not a conspiracy theory, but a serious threat."

Rosella opened the field ops app and filled in a request for a strike against the Church's compound on Gravel Mountain based on the intel from Ranger Newton. The Church violated their Federal lands purchase agreement by bringing in the heavy military weapons, and that was enough to justify the raid, despite the current investigations by the IRS and several states for misappropriated child adoption funding.

IX

While the approvals for the strike request started going through the standard chain of command, Rosella's Assistant Special Agent in Charge, Virginia Hunt, came by Rosella's office to talk.

"Rosella, can we talk about your raid request for Gravel Mountain?" Virginia said, pulling up a chair.

"Sure. Is there something wrong with the request? It seemed straightforward."

"No, the paperwork is in order. But are you sure about this? I am getting heat from the Deputy Chief on this case."

"What? I don't understand. Why would the Deputy Chief be involved?"

"I don't know. He has a copy of the request and has been asking questions about it and its justifications."

"It's a simple, open-and-shut case of term violations with their use of military weapons."

"I know, but the Deputy Chief seems to want to make sure we are sure about this one."

"Oh, come on. Ranger Newton could call in a strike because she was under fire from these people. She has been a witness to them on patrol with military grade weapons. I think we have enough evidence to support probable cause."

"Okay. I wanted to touch base with you about it before I talk with the Deputy Chief." Virginia got up and went back to her office.

X

For reasons unknown, Rosella's raid request took longer than normal to approve, but it went through. In an unusual move, Colonel Cristina Higgins with the Ranger Marshals requested that two companies be assigned to this raid versus the standard one, meaning that Lieutenant Colonel Nishay Powell would be in the field.

As the day of the raid arrived, Rosella thought to herself, "How odd that the Deputy Chief of the ISB was questioning things, but the normal Ranger Marshal brass appears gun-ho on taking on this group since day one. I should stop thinking like this, or I will end up like the old man Bruce, chasing down conspiracy theories all day long."

Three hundred Ranger Marshals flooded the area of Gravel Mountain and overwhelmed the two-armed vehicles of the church's mountain compound.

The church group had hollowed out an entire compound into the Gravel Mountain, and the Ranger Marshal units fanned out in all directions as they entered the large, gated entrance.

Inside there were more fire fights with some leftovers, but the Ranger Marshals dispatched them. Half a dozen men and women were arrested that day.

Once secured, the ISB team entered the complex. The Assistant Special Agent in Charge or ASAC, Virginia Hunt, said to Rosella, "I want you at my side as we go through this place. I have never seen such a large site before. Why did we let this go on so long?"

"Ma'am, according to Ranger Newton, they brought in major heavy equipment to build this place, and yet when I looked at the reports during that time there seemed to be no concern."

As the two traveled through the complex's corridors, Agent Hunt said, "It looks like they were in a rush to get everything out of here. There are a lot of scuff marks on the floor where heavy equipment must have been removed. See here, along the wall, something big and heavy must have banged against it."

"I agree. I could follow up with Ranger Newton to see if she observed any additional traffic showing heavy equipment movement."

The two made their way into a large room. Inside they found evidence of more electrical equipment: wires and connections strewn about. Human size plastic bags with tube connections lie torn on the floor, and some fluid like substance had leaked out.

"We will need a sample of that fluid, but I have a feeling I know what it is already."

"You think it's cloning fluid?" Rosella said, looking at the puddle of goo.

"I think so. This place will take at least a month to process, and I will call in the FBI on this one."

As the two were exiting the large room, a Ranger came up to the ASAC and said, "The Lieutenant Colonel would like to see you Ma'am."

The two of them exited the compound and walked to where the Lieutenant Colonel was standing.

"So, it looks like they bugged out before we could nab them all?" The Lieutenant Colonel said.

"Yes, Ma'am. It appears so," Agent Hunt responded.

"Well, we got a few. But I want you two to see something my *solider girls* found near the compound."

The three of them walked about fifty yards into the woods from the main entrance until they came to a slight clearing which had the ground disturbed. There were five Ranger Marshals standing guard. Upon coming closer, it was obvious the church people dug the ground up and put it back into place. That is when Rosella noticed something poking out from the dirt.

Rosella walked closer to the item, knelt, and then realized it was a small child's hand poking up through the dirt. The hand had cybernetic parts.

Standing back up, Rosella walked back to Agent Hunt and Lieutenant Colonel and said, "We have a mass grave site with cybernetic children in it."

"I thought you two might be interested." Said the Lieutenant Colonel.

"Oh, crap. Now it will take at least two months to process this place." Agent Hunt said out loud as she ran her hand through her short crew cut hair.

"One more thing." The Lieutenant Colonel said, waving to a Ranger who was holding a pod shaped item.

The Ranger walked over to the three women and showed them a foot long, dark plastic oblong shaped object.

The Lieutenant Colonel then spoke, "My tactical unit is uncertain why the hell they scatter these things throughout the woods."

Rosella took the object from the Ranger and looked at it, saying, "Interesting. There seem to be no seams to it. Like it's injected in a mold as a solid piece."

Turning to the Lieutenant Colonel, the ASAC said, "Ma'am, just have your guys gather them all up. I'll have our people, process them for the FBI. I'll make sure you get a full report on the entire investigation once it's done."

Once the Lieutenant Colonel had left, the ASAC said to Rosella, "Special Agent Tolfree, we have our work cut out for us. I despise this Church of the Ember Coalition. I hope this is the last of them."

XI

Back at her office, Rosella sent a message to her old partner, Bruce Daugherty. He was still at the Yosemite National Park Supervisory Office, and hadn't retired yet.

She knew Bruce had amassed a treasure trove of information on Church of the Ember Coalition, even before the Ranger Marshals, when he was a Special Agent with the National Park Service. Rosella recalled him talking about it non-stop when she was assigned to him initially. She had dismissed it as a crazy conspiracy Social Media thing. That was until the ASAC mentioned not liking the Church, and the discovery of Phase and other children.

But all she got back from him was the following brief reply of "Sorry, can't help you. Know nothing about the Ember Coalition or its activities."

"I don't get it. How can someone go from firmly believing that it's something real to 'I know nothing'? Has old age finally caught up with Bruce and dementia has sat in? Well, I don't have anytime to visit him or make any more queries. I'm going to have to use what I got for the report."

XII

Several weeks earlier, Phase laid face up on a steel gurney, being pushed by a thin young man dressed in a full-length white lab coat. Buttoned up on the left side was the lab coat, and it had a right breast pocket but no insignias or company logos on it.

He pushed the metal gurney through some lab doors, where a gray-haired Japanese man wearing black rimmed thick glasses and dressed in a similar lab coat was standing next to a computer terminal.

"Dr. Arai, I have an unusual cybernetic catatonic case."

"Fascinating. I have not seen a cyberpsychosis case in over twenty years. Not since they have banned the use of cerebrum cybernetics." He pulled out a penlight from his right breast pocket and shined it into Phase's eyes, moving it back and forth across his face. As he did, Phase's eyes tracked with the light.

"Yes, an obvious case of Akinetic catatonia. Let me see his records." He asked, putting the penlight back in his lab coat pocket and holding his hand out for the tablet resting on the steel gurney.

Flicking his finger up the tablet's screen, Dr. Arai said, "Interesting. Wyoming. Nanite growth enhancements. Use of preprogrammed, virtual reality A.I." He paused for a moment as he stared at the tablet, then looked up at the young man.

"Are these records accurate? They are showing he is a child of seven years of age, a *clone* product of an A-4 Surrogate, and is a genetic schizophrenic with autism tendencies. These genetic mental issues should have been filtered out."

"Yes sir, we performed the standard genetic blood test on him an hour ago."

"Amazing. Such a young child to have cybernetic implants and mental health issues. There are also still traces of once active nanites in his blood. Do we have parental records from the A-4 Surrogate?"

"No, I am sorry, sir. The National Park Service didn't have those records."

"I see. Place him in the stasis chamber 12 and hook him up for monitoring with an IV drip. Tell Judith I will watch this one."

"Yes, Dr. Arai."

#   #   #   #   #

Gudo Muurling
Founder of the Church of the Ember Coalition

The Demented Augmented Cap

The U.S. Senate Committee Meeting

I

Behind the closed doors of a conference room in the Hart Senate Office Building in Washington, DC, Field Marshal Michael Walden of the U.S. Ranger Marshals, along with Lieutenant Field Marshal Genevieve Duredent, were being grilled by members of the U.S. Senate Intelligence Committee on the current operations of the U.S. Ranger Marshals.

"Field Marshal Walden are you expecting us to believe this ridiculous idea that the Church of the Ember Coalition has infiltrated the highest levels of our government?" the elderly Senator Sara Hobbs said with a stern look upon her face.

"Yes, Ma'am."

"Are you insane? Your reports show their leader died years ago in a hospital in upstate New York, and yet he may still be alive as either a computer A.I. upload or a cybernetic humanoid. Have you read Gudo Muurling's 'proofs' as he calls them?"

"Yes, Ma'am."

"I see. Well, let me read a few quotes for the committee records. And I quote, 'The dough of tomorrow will be the yeast of today.' 'Into the light of the setting sun shall the children of manna go forth to become humanity's gods.' Or my favorite, 'The heads of mankind shall burn with a thousand suns.' This Gudo Muurling is a complete certified nut job, and you're saying his group should be one of the greatest terrorist threats this great nation has ever faced?" Senator Hobbs said as she became flustered and red in the cheeks.

"Ma'am, I believe our intel is solid on this group, and I maintain they are still a major threat. Their exact activities are still unknown. Their leadership structure is unknown, except for the Dutch spiritual founder, Gudo Muurling. A few years ago, they had issues with their tax status and issues with several states over misappropriated adoption funding. Then, as Lieutenant Field Marshal Duredent just testified, we shut down one of their operations in Yellowstone National Park."

Interrupting Field Marshal Walden, Senator Hobbs said, "Yes, let us go over that, shall we? According to the reports the committee received, by the time your group had arrived in the Gravel Mountain complex, the Ember Coalition had already left. The follow up forensics by the FBI showed nothing of significance or connections with any known criminal entities, foreign or domestic. At worst, they may have been operating an illegal cloning operation to supply adoptable children."

"With all respects Ma'am, our own ISB team noted that the mass grave contained children with cybernetic implants." LTFM Duredent said into the mic.

"Well, according to the FBI reports, they showed no cybernetic implants on the bodies of those children. I think your ISB group may need more training."

"Ma'am, with all respects to the FBI, I can't see how it's possible there were no cybernetic implants. The reports from my Lieutenant Colonel, who was in the field, confirmed the ISB Team findings," LTFM Duredent responded.

"Well, they did not forward those reports to this committee." Turning to the Chairperson, Senator Hobbs continued, "Chairperson, I am done with my questioning. I think as a committee we have enough information here to decide about this request. Please dismiss the Field Marshal and Lieutenant Field Marshal."

As Senator Hobbs was the last Senator asking questions, the Chairperson concluded the session and dismissed the Field Marshal and Lieutenant Field Marshal

II

The dry heat of the spring was baking the pavement as the driverless car took the two commanding officers back to the National Headquarters of the Ranger Marshals at I Street NW. As the two sat in the back, while a Ranger sat in the driver's seat position, Lieutenant Field Marshal Duredent commented, "Well, Mike, that could have gone better."

"I know."

"You warned me about Senator Hobbs, but I didn't expect the third degree from her. I thought they only allowed the Senators a certain amount of time for questioning. She started the session, then went again right after the lunch break, and then just now at the end. How did she get so much time?"

"Two things. One: seniority. Two: the other Senators fear her. She is one of the top-ranking Senators right now."

"I can't imagine how you deal with her in the subcommittee or the Appropriations Committee."

Pulling out some antacids from his uniform's pocket, Walden chewed two.

"Migraines?" Duredent asked.

"Just the early symptoms. The doctors prescribed new drugs, but nothing is working. To be honest, there are days I feel like a pregnant woman with all this nausea." Walden joked.

"You should put in for maternity leave then, Mike."

"I would if it would keep me away from Senator Hobbs for nine months."

III

The two commanding officers continued the conversation in the spacious office of the Field Marshal on the seventh floor. "Jenny, I know the Committee will not approve our requests concerning the Ember Coalition. But I still want to keep gathering intel on them."

"I understand."

Walden's face became tense as a crease above his eyebrows showed his concern. "While I don't blame Jane Barker for using us for the Utah secession issue, I have problems with her cabinet."

"It wouldn't have to do with the fact she was the Vice President to Carmela Cordano, who was impeached for money laundering and running a drug cartel?"

"Not so much with Cordano, but Barker likes to court the more radical elements in our society. Groups like the Darwinists, and John Elliott's people."

"John Elliott's group concerns me. In my region they have been giving me trouble on the Indian lands. I tell you they will spark another war with the Sioux nation if they keep up their terrorist-like activities."

"I didn't realize John Elliott's group were terrorizing the Sioux." Walden tried to relax his face, but the weight of these concerns caused his eyebrows to furrow even more. The stress was not helping his developing migraine.

"Mike, it's terrible. They have been doing this hit-and-run scare tactic. Seems to be a bunch of junior members. They drive through a Sioux village at night and shoot in the air. That kind of stuff. We are trying to track down the specific members to arrest them before the Sioux take matters into their own hands."

"Jenny, keep me informed on the developments of this issue. We may have to alert the other regions with tribal areas in case this is some new tactic," the Field Marshal said as he rubbed his temples.

"Is the migraine setting in?"

"Jenny looks like we will cut our visit short. Tell my secretary on the way out if you could?" Walden said, dimming the lights to his office from his desk.

"Not a problem," Duredent said, getting up.

Mell Sutton

IV

Mell Sutton was sitting in his small basement apartment in the refurbished building near what used to be the Fillmore in Silver Spring. He had partially converted it into a 3 D graphics studio for his work. Mell, like most of his generation, was disillusioned with all the political options. He cared less about the issues of android labor taking over human jobs touted by the Sandford Party, or the Democrats. The Republicans offered nothing to his liking. They seemed divided over the whole State of Texas vs. Hanson case, which was causing a big firestorm of debate on the Social Media Net over the right to kill people with guns. Then there were these oddball parties like the Libertarians and the Blue Backer Party offering weird ideas for governance. The funny thing is, no politician seemed to care about the environmental changes happening all around them, such as Florida disappearing into the ocean. Everyone accepted the problems of climate change as just another fact of life, despite that Mell and some voters still thought it was important. So, Mell just tuned out the political side of society and poured himself into his work of constructing 3-D terrains and landscapes for video games and the latest immersion reality systems of the Social Media Net.

Mel had saved up on getting an augmented cap installed under the skin of his head. These pieces of technology allowed him to access his computer systems without the use of special 3-D glasses or goggles. Augmented computer images fed into the visual and hearing centers of his cerebral cortex. Those who could afford this piece of technology either played games with it, or in Mell's case used it for 3-D graphic engineering and modeling.

For Mell, one feature he could turn off was the pop-up ads embedded in the surrounding environment.

Before he learned how to disable this feature, it was most disturbing to be going about your business and then have this 3-D animated cartoon-like mascot jump out at you, usually offering you some product from a nearby restaurant or store.

V

One very early morning, the call of a woman's voice awakened Mell.

"Mell. Mell. It's time to get up." The female voice called out.

"Uh? What?" Mell sat up with the sheets wrapped around his thin, lanky frame.

Rubbing the sleep from his eyes, he noticed standing next to his bed a woman dressed in a green skintight dress with a slit up the left side.

"Wait? Who are you?"

"I am Songbird. It's time for you to get up." "Songbird? I don't understand."

"It's okay. Some disorientation is to be expected." "Disorientation? What are you talking about?" The confused

Mel sat on the edge of his bed in his underwear.

"Mell, you have a big day ahead of you. You still must finish that project for the Gao De Gaming Group," said Songbird as she walked towards the door.

"Yeah. The Gao De project. I am almost done with it," Mell said, rubbing his head as he stood up from the bed.

"Why don't you get dressed and get something to eat. Then start on the project."

"Sounds good, Songbird." Said Mell as he lumbered over to a pile of clothing sitting on top of a dresser.

VI

At first Mell thought Songbird was an interactive productivity app he downloaded and forgot. He ran internal diagnostics on his augmented cap and all were fine. He thought about deleting the Songbird program, but in the end didn't because he found it so useful. As the week rolled on, Songbird kept making suggestions to Mell on ways to improve his life from his diet to his sleeping habits, to how to spend his time. Mell became more accepting of Songbird's ideas as the program stayed on.

"Mell, become a vegan. A total vegan diet would be the best thing for you. It would improve your mental health."

"I didn't know that. Songbird, I don't know why, but I find you so wise."

At night, Songbird would chant Mel to sleep. As the weeks rolled on into a month, Mel had never felt so satisfied in his life. Everything seemed so perfect with Songbird. Songbird kept him on track by keeping him awake. She helped him with food choices in the store. Songbird instructed him to remove all the forks and knives but keep all the spoons. She sang him to sleep each night. Life could not be more ideal.

VII

The Voice of Stacey

My name is Stacey, and I was born in the Great Flooded Salt Marsh of New Jersey. No one is supposed to live there, but people do. We were refugees and social outcasts from society during the Great Melt. We formed small communities named Cranbury, Applegarth, and Windsor. The State House of New Jersey in Frankford of the Northern Hill Lands didn't care about us living in the Great Flood Salt Marsh. I think no one knew about us. We had our own ways, society and laws - laws based on keeping to oneself and not bothering with anyone else unless it was for trade. My birth mother's trade was that of pleasing people, and that is how we lived from day to day. Both men and women would visit us for trade.

It was there my birth mother met my gene-mother; they fell in love and had me. My gene-mother died when I was three. I recall little about her except that she was old.

When I was sixteen, the Paddyrollers took away my birth mother. They only wanted her because she was contraband android property with a warrant for her retrieval. Being a human clone, the Paddyrollers didn't want me and left me on my own. I left the Great Flooded Salt Marsh and made my way to the old bridges of Trenton. The people who lived there were kind, and I repaid them with my flesh as my mother taught me. From there I made my way south towards Baltimore and then towards the Nation's Capital. Those who I stayed with in Baltimore told me that a girl like me would do well with the legislators. I am now nineteen years old, and this skinny man wants me to come with him back to his place.

So, I went with him, like I had done with the other men and women in all the other communities. I saw no difference in him than any other person I had met so far.

His place was a small basement apartment, but it was so nice to get off the streets, even if it was just for a single night. The hot weather was becoming unbearable. He said his name was Mell. He talked to himself a lot, but I had seen that before, so that wasn't something new.

When I first arrived at his apartment, while he put away the small bag of groceries he had, I undressed myself thinking I was going to please him right away. That is how it goes. But he was different. As I stood there in my panties, he grabbed my neck and threw me down onto his sofa saying, "I am not after sex! Now get dressed!" Mell scared me.

My birth mother had told me a little about the dark ways of pleasing people, but I had never experienced it before. I lay there rubbing my neck as my chest heaved with fright. I got up and dressed myself. For a good while I stood there in the middle of the room while Mell sat at his small dining table eating a bowl of soup. He stared at me with these sunken eyes with each spoonful. Sunken eyes I hadn't noticed before that made me uneasy. I wondered why I came to this man. I knew, though, if he would let me, please him, he would let me go. That's how it's supposed to work. I felt too scared to just leave.

The people in Baltimore always said to carry a phone or infopad with you because there are crazy people out there, but I couldn't afford one, and the Government had stopped the free phone program years ago when they put the flood refugees into camps. So, I just stood there struck with fear; wishing he would just let me pleasure him so I could leave.

VIII

For the next two weeks, Mell kept Stacey in his basement apartment as Songbird told him what to do. When Mell had to go out, he would lock the outside door in such a way that Stacey couldn't unlock it to leave. Stacey tried to befriend Mel using the only way she knew how; by trying to please him like her birth mother had taught her. She hoped by befriending him he might let her go. She had never encountered a person like Mel before and was unsure what to do. Her birth mother never told her what to do with people like Mel.

"Don't you like me? It looks like you like me," Stacey said one morning looking at Mell sitting on the edge of his bed in his underwear.

"I told you. I don't want sex from you. So put your clothes back on again," Mell said, staring at the naked, half-emaciated 19-year-old girl.

It had been a long while since Mell had dated or had sex, since embarking on his lonely career of doing 3-D computer renderings for gaming companies. Songbird was much more attractive to him. She wasn't emaciated and was much taller.

Songbird was perfect in every way. A much more real woman to Mell than Stacey could be.

Songbird would tell Mell that this young woman will be a trial for Poduna, Goddess of Miracles. "

"Mell when the time comes, Poduna will demand from you this young woman. You must be strong."

"I will be strong, Songbird."

"Soon you will join the others at the Gathering. Then Poduna will reveal herself."

"I await the Miracles of Poduna!" Mell would scream out loud.

IX
The Voice of Stacey Continued

Mell scares me. He will go about yelling, 'I await the Miracles of Poduna'. I asked him once who Poduna was, and he grabbed me around my neck and choked me. I told him he was hurting me as I struggled against his grip, and he let go.

He keeps mentioning that I am to be a trial for Poduna. I don't understand what he means by that. I want to leave this place. He locks the door in such a way so I can't open it. When he leaves, I've banged on the door to the point my hands hurt, but no one comes. The one little window has bars on it and I can't even open it or break the glass. He has computer stuff he works by day and night, but I cannot make it work. My birth mother never taught me about such things.

Once when he was gone, I screamed for help until my throat was sore, but no one came. I thought I could find maybe a weapon, but he has no knives or forks. Just spoons for his vegetable soup. That is all he must eat: pouches of vegetable soup. His computers don't even have cords I could use. He locks the door all the time. He is up most of the time and does not sleep. Once when he was asleep, I approached him, and he woke up. I see no way to get away from him.

I feel like the dog my gene-mom had tied up around the tree. I was young then, but I can still remember this skinny dog tied up to a tree. It would eat pretty much anything we gave it. I remember it dying with this painful yelp. Everything in that swamp just died. That is why I had to leave after the Paddyrollers took my birth mother; although, now I fear this basement has become my new swamp, and Mell is the rope tied to the tree like that dog. I have tried to befriend him like how my birth mother showed me, but he will have nothing of it. He keeps yelling at me to get dressed. I think he wants me to please him, at least that is what his pants are showing when I am naked in front of him. But he keeps saying no and pushes me away, or worse, grabs me by the throat.

X

"Mell. Mell. It's time for the trial. Get up, Mell." "What? Songbird is that you?"

"Yes, Mell. It's Songbird. Get up. It's time for Poduna's trial." Mell got up out of his bed and got dressed. He stood in the middle of his room with his hands in the air, prayerfully awaiting.

"Mell, now go forth and buy a gun. Poduna wants you to own a gun."

"Yes, Songbird."

So, Mell left his basement apartment while Stacey was asleep. He purchased an automatic handgun and a box of ammunition. Since the Federal Appeals Court decision of State of Texas vs. Hanson, the purchasing of firearms and ammunition had become a lot easier with no waiting time imposed by the federal government.

When he returned, Mell began to clean the gun as directed by Songbird.

XI
The Voice of Stacey Final

I didn't realize Mell had left until I saw him sitting at the dining table with a gun. He must have just bought the thing while I was asleep. He will shoot me dead. I know he will shoot me dead.

His bedroom. I could try to hide in his bedroom until he runs out of bullets. But he has so many in that carton on the table.

The Paddyrollers had guns. That is how they could take my birth mother away, by shooting her in the leg. But Mell will do worse.

Why couldn't he let me pleasure him and then let me go?

Like the others. Why did he have to be like the Paddyrollers?

XII

Mell had finished putting the gun back together for the eighth time, he stood up and walked over to Stacey, who was sitting on the edge of the sofa.

Stacey was frozen. Not sure what to do as Mell walked with intent towards her, she bolted towards Mell's bedroom in an instant.

Mell lunged at her, grabbed her neck from behind, and then threw her back onto the sofa with such force she bounced off the cushions.

Stacey then tried to get back up again, but as she did, she found the weight of Mell on top of her small body pinning her to the sofa.

Then Mell choked her with both of his hands pressing downwards. Stacey grabbed his forearms and tried as hard as she could to kick at him.

She was gagging. Stacey tried to shake her head back and forth to free herself from his grasp, but it only got tighter. She scratched at him with her freed hands, but he pushed harder against her throat and adjusted his position to be on top of her chest.

Tears were welling up in her eyes. She could see this distorted blank stare on Mel's face through them, as a pounding headache developed in her head. She was finding it harder to struggle and move. Her lungs burned. Her lips were turning blue.

She closed her eyes and spots of lights flashed. Then darkness, and she became limp, struggling no more.

"Don't let go, Mell. You must hold on to her for a little longer. She can still come back."

"Yes, Songbird." Mell said as he sat on top of the now dead Stacey, still choking her blue-lipped corpse.

XIII

Stacey's corpse laid on the sofa while Mell went to rent a self-driving U-cart automobile. When he got back with the U-cart, he first loaded the gun and ammo into the passenger side of the front seat of the car, then he wrapped Stacey's corpse up in one of his bed blankets and threw her small body over his shoulder. No one noticed Mell loading Stacey's small body into the back seat of the self-driving car in broad daylight. Downtown Silver Spring, Maryland was desolate with a few buildings and stores left since the County began its reclamation. Lower Montgomery County was being turned back towards farmland and parks to create a buffer zone for the ever rising waters of the ocean despite the levee built to protect the Nation's Capital. Getting into the front driver seat, Songbird whispered to Mell the coordinates to punch in for the car.

The car drove around the Capital Beltway and exited at Connecticut Ave., making a left onto Beach Drive. The driverless car went for about 1,000 feet down Beach Drive and then stopped, saying in a pleasant female voice, "You have arrived at your destination. Do you still plan to use U-cart for further transportation needs?"

"Tell it, yes," said Songbird to Mell.

"Yes, please stay here," Mell instructed the car, as he got out and went to the rear driver-side door.

He pulled Stacy's sheet-wrapped body out of the car and slung it over his shoulder. He then walked about one hundred feet towards Rock Creek and dumped her body on the ground. Songbird told him to cover it up with some fallen branches that lay nearby, although the white sheet was a dead give-away.

"Good enough. Let us go to the others, Mell," Songbird whispered into Mell's ears.

"To the Gathering! I await the Miracles of Poduna!" Mel said with his arms raised in prayer.

"Before you get in, grab that mushroom over there. You need something to eat." Songbird said, pointing to a mushroom on the ground.

"Poduna provides!" Mell yelled, grabbing a bright, orange-colored mushroom on a nearby log and eating it.

Songbird gave Mell the coordinates to the next destination, and the car drove on its way.

Rosella's Investigation

XIV

The government-issued self-driving car came to a stop on Beach Drive, and Special Agent Rosella Tolfree got out. The heat of the spring day was not helping the crime scene that was a few hundred feet away from her. She could smell that stench of death as she saw the Montgomery County Homicide and Investigative Units dealing with the covered bloated corpse.

Captain Tammy Manger-Jung came up to Rosella, "This makes the eighth death in Rock Creek this past quarter. Are you sure you don't want me to get the FBI involved? These are federal lands."

"Not yet. All the Rock Creek murders are still under my jurisdiction. What have your investigative teams put together so far?" Rosella asked, holding her nose as the two approached closer.

"Well, all are female. They appear to be of varying ages from a teen to an elderly woman in her late 80s. The only common thread is they appear to have been strangled to death, at least that is what the coroner is showing at this point. There is a lack of physical evidence in each case for the exact cause of death except asphyxiation. There doesn't appear to be any sexual assault either prior or after."

"Have you been able to put together a list of suspects?" Rosella asked as she looked at the extended stomach of the small woman in a summer dress.

"We thought we were dealing with a serial killer at first, but there were too many unconnected things with each death. We couldn't get the victims to line up with any pattern or with cold cases that were out there. Each victim, so far, seems to be random and unconnected with each other. If it is a serial killer, we don't understand how he or she is getting the victims and how they are being selected or targeted. We have also found nothing on the Social Media Net of the identified victims to point to any one person or suspicious activity."

Leaning against a tree, Rosella brushed away a strand of her red hair from her face, saying to the captain, "We're missing something that ties them all together. Some element that links each victim to their killer." Pulling herself from the tree, Rosella walked back to her car, saying to the captain, "Keep me informed of any new developments."

XV

Rosella got back in her driverless car and told it to take her back to the ISB Field Office on I Street, NW. As the car was driving back, she grabbed her tactical infopad and started reviewing the murder case information from the Montgomery County Police.

Rosella would have turned these cases over to the FBI, with her just pushing the paperwork for the Ranger Marshals. Something inside her told her not to do that with the first one. There had been something odd about the first death, and something odd about all eight deaths. The rate of first-degree murders had been declining over the years as more men left to work in space colonies, leaving a female majority on Earth. Yet something told her these murders were premeditated, despite the sloppy nature of the body disposal and the wide variety of ages. To make matters worse, each corpse had decayed to a point where a good chromophore scan from their eyes wasn't possible.

"Could we be dealing with a new serial killer?" Rosella said to herself as she flicked her finger across the infopad.

She looked at the arrangement of known addresses for six of the victims and had the tactical infopad's investigation app try to trace patterns between the points. Nothing was coming up - no stars, no cryptic symbols, nothing.

"Maybe it was in the street names?" She said to herself as she ran the street names through the app.

"Damn it! Nothing." She said in frustration as the app came back with gibberish.

"Maybe there is something with that first case." She said to herself as she pulled up the file. A sixteen-year-old girl from Gaithersburg had gone missing after attending a student get-together at a local restaurant. Montgomery County police records show that the teen girl was last seen with her older cousin, but when County police questioned the older cousin, he said she had gone home by herself.

Rosella compared this first case to each of the other remaining five cases with known addresses. Then she noticed something: in each of the cases, the victim was last seen in the presence of a male. She thought this was odd as she said to herself, "Why are all the last people seen with the victim a male? Each one can't be the killer? Are these copycat killers? But we haven't seen copycat killers in years, thanks to advances in drug therapy."

"But this seventh death is different. She was a Jane Doe. The Montgomery County Police suspected she was probably a prostitute or street person based on the health conditions of the corpse. I wonder if that is what we will see with death number eight as well? Has the patterned changed to unrelated people?" Rosella asked herself as the driverless car made its way into the parking garage.

Rosella sat in her driverless car after it parked itself, just staring at the tactical infopad saying to herself, "The ISB doesn't have the resources for murder cases. Why am I bothering with these cases? Why am I going to the ASAC? I have been stringing him out for the last calendar quarter with these cases. Maybe the Montgomery County Police Captain is right, and I should just let the FBI handle everything. They are better equipped to investigate murder cases like this than the ISB. I have to depend upon local resources for all my information, while the FBI has their own labs. Maybe I am way in over my head on this one. But I feel that something seems so familiar about them. I can't figure it out yet. Sometimes I wish Bruce was still here. He always ha such insight into these kinds of cases."

XVI

Rosella took the elevator to the fifth floor and walked amidst the cubicles to hers. She sat down in front of her smoke-glass monitor, which faced a large glass window looking out towards Franklin Square. She turned to a small fish tank sitting on the side, saying to the small goldfish swimming about, "Hubert, it is way too hot outside for you. You would just dry up in an instant."

Rosella was working on paperwork for the rest of the day when she got an e-message from the Montgomery County Police Captain on the recent death. It was, as Rosella had suspected, another Jane Doe. As she read through the preliminary Corner report, it showed that the victim was a nineteen-year-old clone from an A-4 android, based on the genetic imprinting. Like all female clones, the young woman was genetically modified so as not to have children, and based on her gene sequence, she was from an elderly set of human genes. She also showed serious signs of early malnutrition from height and weight issues to some brain anomalies suggesting possible mental illness. She also showed clear and repeated sexual contact since a young age and somehow contracted an STD which had not impacted her.

"An A-4 clone? Why is a malnourished A-4 clone being murdered in a park? It's like someone was trying to make the ideal human prostitute using an A-4 cloning system. But what is the connection to the others? Why the change in victim?" Rosella said to herself as she leaned back in her swivel chair.

Then leaning forward again, Rosella had a flash of inspiration; she quickly pointed to the programs she was working on and saved and closed them out. She then pulled up the investigative app, grabbed the keyboard from the desk, locked the swivel chair's wheels, and leaned back again in the swivel chair as she put her feet up against the edge of the desk, resting the keyboard in her lap. In a scrunched-up position, she typed and move the cursor ball about as window after window scrolled by on the smoke- colored glass screen.

"What if there was something with each of the earlier victims that required a change in victim type? Something that would tip us police people off. And there it is!" She said with excitement as the app found a common element between all the earlier victims. The application showed that the males who were last seen with each victim had become a missing person themselves.

"Each person had a reasonable alibi, the county cleared each person as a suspect, and then they become a missing person. But what is the connection between them all? They are each just so different. It's like I am dealing with a third unknown person they all know.

"I wonder how many other recent murders there have been in the Atlantic Field Office region with the same killing style?" Rosella said to herself as she typed into the app's system.

Another eight victims showed up from western Maryland to West Virginia to Virginia. All the victims were female; all were varying ages, just like the ones in Rock Creek Park. But they had turned these cases over to the FBI for processing, and Rosella could not pull up any additional information as each case was now closed out in the Investigative Service Branch's systems.

Rosella tried to access the cases using her credentials with the FBI's systems, but it denied her access.

Tossing the keyboard onto the desk and stamping her feet to the ground as she came to a normal sitting position in her swivel chair, she said, "What the fuck! Damn FBI!"

Rosella sat as she twisted a lock of her red hair around her left index finger, lost in thought about what to do next. Then it came to her. She got up and headed for the elevator.

XVII

Rosella took the elevator to the garage and went to her driverless car. Getting in the car, she grabbed the tactical infopad and pulled up the net investigation app on the infopad. "God, I hope this doesn't get me into too much trouble. I mean, there is nothing like hacking your own organization."

She sat in her car for about an hour typing away on the tactical info pad, and not paying attention to the heat of the day, until she got what she was after. "I knew the raw data had to still be available in those cases somewhere in the system. There is always a backup living somewhere." She said with joy in her voice.

Downloading the data into the infopad, she said, "Okay, let's see what else we have on those cases that went to the FBI."

Reviewing the data. Seven of the people who were last seen with each of these victims were female and only one was male. "How odd. I expected the last person seen with each one to be all males."

Digging deeper into the data, she crossed the list of last seen people with local reported missing, and each one showed up as missing.

With one of the missing people on the list, there was additional information she could access. She pulled up the records from the local municipality. "Says here she was last seen driving away in a U-cart. According to the main file, she owned her own car. So, why would a woman who owns a car just rent one?"

Rosella then used her ISB credentials to access the U-cart system and then crossed indexed the list of last seen people with their rental records. "What? All of them rented a U-cart? I have to see the routes of these U-carts."

She had the tactical infopad apps pull up all the driving information from the various rented U-carts and then map them all out. The paths showed them going to the park locations, then leaving the park locations and heading towards Sugar Grove, West Virginia.

"What the hell is in Sugar Grove, West Virginia? And I wonder if there are any more U-carts going there from federal parks?"

She continued to access the U-cart database as she sat in her car, realizing that it was getting hot. Beads of sweat were rolling down her face and dripping onto the infopad. "Damn spring heat." She said, turning on the car's air conditioning system, while wiping the infopad with her hand.

"There you two are." She said seeing the last two U-carts that lined up with her two Jane Does.

Rosella now had a complete list of renters who lined up with all sixteen victims. The U cart renters all went to a destination outside of Sugar Grove, West Virginia after strangling a woman. Seven of them were women, and nine were men. But she still had no actual connection between them, except that they were all under the age of thirty-five years.

She looked at the last one, Mell Sutton. A 3-D computer graphics renderer. He was the oldest of the bunch. Looking in the standard criminal database, it had nothing on him, just like the others. They were all normal people. "Why would normal people kill women? How does Sugar Grove fit into all this?" she said, twisting a lock of her red hair around her finger.

"I need to do a wider Social Media Net search on these people." Rosella said as she pulled up the Net Investigation App and continued, saying, "There has to be a connection between them all. Something common to them all."

She fed the list of U-cart renters into the app and let it loose upon the Social Media Net. In a few minutes the app was categorizing results between all except Mell Sutton. Fifteen of those on the list were computer game players who played together in socially augmented reality games or other social game platforms. Mell was working for various computer game manufacturers as one of the chief graphic designers for the backgrounds for some games the other fifteen played. "They are all social gamers? But what's with Sugar Grove?"

She investigated the Sugar Grove connection and discovered that near the little town there was an old NSA satellite dish location that had been sold off when the NSA was dissolved. It was sold to a now defunct social net media company, according to the IRS records. The land was transferred back to federal control once the company went under, but it still listed the site as abandoned according to federal records and under the Ranger Marshals' jurisdiction.

"So, I have sixteen social gamers all traveling to an abandoned NSA satellite dish location. Is this supposed to be the largest social gaming hack of all time? And why kill a bunch of women in the process? None of this makes sense, except I know where the killers are, and I have enough information to process a raid request."

XVIII

Rosella got out of her car and went back upstairs to her cubicle. She filed the paperwork for a raid request against the abandoned NSA satellite dish location in Sugar Grove, WV.

It would be close to a week later that she heard from Jacoby Jaren Datu-imam (J.D.) Sarte, the Assistant Special Agent in Charge or ASAC of the Atlantic Field Office Region in a video e-conference with her.

"Look, Special Agent Tolfree, that was top-notch investigative work, but you can't hold back murder cases from the FBI for months like that. My God, woman, you had eight deaths in one quarter sitting on your desk."

"I know. But I knew I could solve them without their help. The local police around here have sufficient resources for me to do the standard investigative work needed, and the rest I can do on my own. It's like it was when I was out in California years ago."

"That's great, but that's not how we do it in the Atlantic Field Office. We turn over murder cases to the FBI to further investigate. That's final, do you understand?"

"Yes, sir."

"Now, as for the raid request, Quantico will handle the complete field work on this one. The ISB is sitting this one out at their request."

"What?! Quantico?! After all my hard work, and the FBI is getting the collar on this one?"

"Yes. Quantico."

Crossing her arms in a huff, Rosella said, "Whatever."

The ASAC continued to debrief Rosella on what was happening with the case and his expectations of her with it. While the FBI was involved in the criminal investigative side of the case, the actual raid was still being performed by the Ranger Marshals. It was clear to Rosella that she was being disciplined for not following protocol.

Rosella's investigative curiosity of what was at the Sugar Grove site was getting the better of her, and she approached the "weapon girls" as she called them in the sub-basement level of the building to see if she could hook herself up into the vest camera feeds. If she couldn't be there, she wanted to at least see what was going on.

IX

On the day of the raid, Rosella was at home sitting on her love seat in her Takoma Neighborhood Apartment in Washington, DC. She got her tactical infopad to broadcast the live feed from one of the vest cameras in the raid to her wall screen.

"If the ASAC asks about this, I am just going to tell him I needed it for the report." She told herself as she forked into her mouth leftover General Tso from the night before.

As Rosella watched the grainy feed, it reminded her of the old military ops training vids they showed during the basic training. The gray images were out of focus, and every time it looked at a person their eyes were bright dots even in daylight. "One would have thought by now chest cameras would have improved, but I guess not." She said cramming another sauce- soaked fake-chicken bit into her mouth.

The feed showed the Rangers moving through the forest around the Sugar Grove site. Then she heard a crackle sound over the comm and the faint words of "We are taking fire."

Rosella asked the wall unit to turn up the sound, and as she did, she watched and heard the beginnings of a firefight. "Oh, my God! They have guns! Where did they get the guns?" Rosella said to herself.

Rosella continued to watch as the fire fight unfolded before her, she could hear the social gamers yelling "Protect the Statue of Poduna! Stop the unbelievers!"

"What the hell? Is this some insane cult? Who the hell is Poduna?" Rosella said to herself, watching the action unfold before her eyes.

Soon she lost the feed and, grabbing her tactical infopad, she tried to re-establish the connection, but she couldn't. Although not satisfied, Rosella realized that what she saw was about as close to the action as she would get that day.

Flopping backwards, she stretched her short frame out on the love seat and lay there thinking to herself, "Who is Poduna? Why is that name so familiar? Where have I heard that name before? Poduna. Poduna. Poduna.

"Wait a minute, now I remember. I was seven. Poduna was part of this computer game my dad got me."

Grabbing her tactical infopad, she looked up Poduna. The information that came back was Poduna, the Goddess of Miracles, was an early social gaming app where people went around protecting certain worship sites from evil creatures who would want to destroy them. Each player had to perform a test of strength before becoming a champion to protect the site. "So, these social gamers were playing the game in real-life? Or was there some crazy cult based on the game? I guess I will go with the latter for the report when I get back to work, since the FBI will oversee the investigation. If the admins want crap, that is what they will get, crap." She said to herself, tossing the infopad aside and flopping back down on the love-seat.

#   #   #   #   #

USRM-ISB Installment 4 (Rosella's age- 43)

The Marsha Unit

I

Special Agent Rosella Tolfree had her self-driving car park along Perry Street NE of Fort Bunker Hill Park. She had just finished a case near the Monongahela National Forest involving some crazed group of fanatics using an old NSA satellite station, and now she was being assigned to some murders in the Nation's Capital. The FBI would handle this, but according to her Assistant Special Agent in Charge (ASAC) the FBI didn't want to be bothered because it's involving Congress. "The FBI doesn't want to have too much news on the Social Media Net right now as they are trying to have certain budget items passed." The ASAC told her in the video e-message about the case. Rosella found this odd, because it's required that murders involving members of Congress be investigated by the FBI, with other agencies only acting in an assisting capacity. "What help can I provide? I lack a crime lab and other resources the FBI's DC Field Office possesses, " Rosella thought to herself.

On the way over from the downtown office, Rosella reviewed the file that was sent from the DC Metropolitan Police Criminal Investigation Unit, which showed three victims in the last month. There wasn't much detail in the files. All under the age of thirty, and all in the same park. All of them attached to Congress in some fashion. She also glanced through reports filed by US Park Police Officer Reno Ellis, who was the first responder on the scene for the last two; this third one she was going to be a report from the DC Metropolitan Police, but Officer Ellis was still the first responder on the scene.

Rosella pulled her overcoat from the car as a cold rain came down. Up a wooded hill, she could see in the near distance the standard police tape and the gaggle of police investigators.

Arriving at the top of the hill, they directed her to the local Criminal Investigation Detective in charge, Jazmin Koch.

"So, this makes number three in this park?" Rosella asked.

"And you are?"

"Special Agent Rosella Tolfree with the ISB. I was just assigned to these three murder cases." Rosella said, showing her badge and identification.

"So, the FBI is not getting involved?"

"No, the FBI is tied up with congressional budget issues."

"That explains the new blackout request from them. Well, it is their loss, because when this one gets out, they may have a hard time getting things passed." Jazmin said as she pulled up the blue tarp covering the body.

"Isn't that Congressman Buckley of Alabama?!"

"Yeah. Not a pretty sight. He had his genitals ripped off from his groin. Beats the first guy, I guess, where they were bitten off, or the lady where she had her breasts ripped from her chest. We are hoping though to get a good chromophore scan from his eyes since he is naked, and it's cold out."

"I would like a copy of the image if you got something." Rosella said as she took the tarp from Jazmin to look at the body. "Can I ask if you found his genitals?"

"Yeah, they were about ten feet from his head."

"So, they were thrown?"

"Maybe. But that is not what killed him. If you notice, the

perp smashed his right temple in, and the rock that did it is next to his head."

"Wow, that's some serious blunt force trauma. The amount of force needed to do that is impressive. I would like to know from the coroner how many blows it took to smash his skull in like that."

"Sure. I'll make sure you get the report. Look, our team will wrap up here soon. Is there anything else?"

"Is Officer Ellis still here?"

"He is over there boasting like usual." Jazmin said, pointing over to a tall young Black male US Park Police Officer in an animated conversation with two local female DC Metropolitan Police.

Walking past police tape, she approached Officer Ellis, who was making a gun motion with his hand, as he was explaining where he apprehended a perp robbing a local convenience store. "Officer Ellis, could I have a word with you? I am Special Agent Rosella Tolfree with the ISB." She said as she stepped around some mud.

Turning around to face Rosella, Officer Ellis said, "Excuse me ladies, it seems I have a little redheaded fan here."

"Excuse me? Look, I am not your fan, I'm an investigator. I just need some questions answered right now."

The six-foot one Ellis stood his ground with an emotionless look. Brushing her now wet, hair from her face, she said, "Okay, I don't have time for this kind of nonsense. It is raining, and these cases have to be solved. So, you were the first responder in each of them. Does the Park Police maintain any surveillance in the park? Are you using any routine field cameras in the trees?"

Laughing a bit, Officer Ellis responded, "Are you kidding me?! We don't have that kind of budget. You Ranger Marshals eat up all the department's federal funds with your fancy tanks and helicopter gunships. I am lucky to have a self-driving car."

Wiping a wet strand of hair again from her face, "Look, we are all on the same side here. We are a team on the same mission. I can't help how the admins spend the funding. The ISB doesn't have the resources to chase down a murder case, but that's what I am being asked to do. I can take by your response that the park has no additional surveillance."

"You got it, sister. The only surveillance is yours." Officer Ellis laughed.

"Well thanks for your help. I'll be in touch if I need anything else."

As Rosella made her way back to her car, she glanced around to get a feel for the park. It was a large secluded area with lots of woods. The perfect place for pretty much any illicit activity, with a long history of having crimes being done in the park from drugs to rape.

The rain came down in sheets along Perry Street NE just as she got into the car. "I hope DC Criminal Investigation got all they needed because any forensics on the ground are going to be washed away now."

II

Rosella's driverless car was making its winding way back through the one-way streets of downtown DC. All the way back to the I Street NW Field Office next to the Franklin Square Complex, the National Headquarters of the Ranger Marshals.

As the October showers poured, she sat there wondering about the connections of the three individuals. "Why this one particular park?" she thought as she rummaged through some old Chinese food cartons for her tactical infopad.

Pulling up the case file information again, she tried to take a fresh look at the personal data of each victim.

Victim One- Alfonso Chicote (Hispanic, male, 28),
Congressional aide for Representative Christina Oliver (I- CA)

Victim Two- Jodi Harrington (white, female, 23),
Congressional intern for Senator Connie Wheeler (D- PA)

Victim Three- Representative Clifford Buckley (white,
male, 26) (I- AL) (one of the youngest serving representatives
currently). It is known that he has a live-in lover by the name of
Leo Kent (Asian, Male, 30).

Aside from all being connected to Congress, she wasn't seeing anything else. None of them even lived close to the park. The aide and intern lived in Northern Virginia, and Rep. Buckley had an apartment in Georgetown. The park was at least a twenty minute drive from the Capital area where they all would work, and out of their way. The Brookland neighborhood wasn't known for a lot of Congressional workers frequenting it, since it was the site of several private colleges and universities. She could see the intern, but the intern was coming from Northern Virginia, not any of the colleges in Brookland.

As she was stopped at a light, she got an e-message from Detective Jazmin Koch. It contained the eye scan results and some information on some shoe prints that were missing in the original reports provided.

Pulling up the eye scan from Representative Buckley, the image was just a blurry shadowy humanoid figure standing over him. The person appeared small to Rosella, but it could also have been an issue with the scan itself as these eye scans were not that reliable.

Next, she reviewed the shoe print information that was taken at each crime scene. DC Metropolitan Police Criminal Investigation could connect all the shoes present except a size one woman's shoe. According to the report filed by Detective

Koch, the DC Metropolitan Police was focused on a pair of military boot prints which were connected to Troy Bentley, a local Neo-Obliteration Movement member living in the Brookland neighborhood. Mr. Bentley was their lead suspect.

Rosella thought to herself, "A size one female shoe? That's a tiny shoe size. Are we dealing with some sort of odd sex fetish? Or is this just a small prostitute? But no person I know could rip off body parts or smash in a person's head in with rocks. This is unnatural somehow and makes little sense for a Neo-Obliteration Member to kill like this. This is not what they do. Sure, they kill people, but they just shoot them or hang them after a KKK rally or when some known hate supporter gets elected to a town. Not like this, where a person is hunted down in a wooded park. It doesn't fit their manifesto."

III

The self-driving car parked itself in the underground garage of the Ranger Marshal Headquarters, and Rosella took the elevator to the fifth floor. She made her way through the maze of glass-topped Government issued cubicles to hers, which faced a window showing Franklin Square. Rosella's cubicle was all that comprised the DC Field Office of the ISB, but at least it was her office. Around her were various workers associated with the administration work of the U.S. Ranger Marshals. They were the bean counters that kept all the field offices and agents operating, despite being despised for not approving financial requests.

Sheets of rain were just washing down the windows as she turned to her small fish tank on her desk. The fish tank had a small goldfish swimming about it, and she said, "Hubert, I bet you would love to be flopping about out there right now with all this rain. Well, I better check in and begin the reporting on this case. It is such a drag having to come all the way back to the office to do this work. If these accounting trolls would just let my tactical infopad have the needed apps, it would make my life so much easier. But then where would I put you?"

Rosella had pulled up the case app on the smoke-glass monitor standing on her desk before the keyboard and entered some basic information, when Maurice stopped by her cubicle. "Hey, the Big Guy's secretary was down here earlier looking for you. He wants to see you up in his office." Maurice said, leaning on the cubicle's entrance.

Closing out the app, she spun her chair around to face Maurice, "The Field Marshall wants to see me? What for? Did his secretary say why?" Rosella was concerned because this would be the second time in a year she met the Field Marshal, with the first time when she was assigned to the DC Field Office. It was unusual for such a high-ranking official to ask to see someone so low in the ranks, except on special occasions or events.

"No. He said nothing. Just that you need to go up and see him. Maybe it is about a promotion?"

"I wish. I just hope it is not some transfer to a remote field office, like Puerto Rico or Guam."

"Hey now, I would love to go to Guam. I would love to do some drug cartel stuff. That would be great." Maurice said with a bit of excitement in his voice.

"Are you kidding me? You are just an accountant." Rosella said while straightening her field jacket to look professional.

"Hey now. I have the rank of Ranger like many of the others on the floor and a permit to carry a gun."

"Whatever accountant troll, just tell me when you catch your first perp so I can buy you a celebration cupcake," Rosella said as she headed for the elevator.

Rosella took the elevator to the seventh floor, where it opened up to a lobby area.

She exited the elevator and approached the large oak doors of the Field Marshal's Office.

Opening one of the two doors, she saw the uniformed Ranger who was the Field Marshal's secretary sitting behind a small desk across from some cushioned chairs.

"You can go straight in. The Field Marshal has expected your return." The secretary said as he pressed something under his desk.

Rosella entered through another set of oak doors opposite the first into the spacious office of the Field Marshal. The Field Marshal had turned the lights down so that his form was just framed against the glass window wall behind his modest desk. He was staring out the window as the rain poured down toward the Washington Monument to the right of the panel frames.

"I must beg your pardon for the lights being turned down right now, but my migraines are acting up." The Field Marshal said as he continued, "I was wondering, Special Agent Tolfree, do you know how many times people have tried to ram cars into that monument?"

"About six times in the last year alone, sir. Each time they tried to modify the AI programing of the driverless car they were using." Rosella said as she sat down in one of the two chairs in front of his desk.

"What was the modus operandi of each case?"

"They all were part of some anarchist group trying to exercise what they think is their right to express their free speech as a political demonstration."

"And part of our duty is to protect that monolithic rock from being smashed by people with cars and protect their rights to free speech."

"Sir, I don't think one's right to free speech includes property destruction."

"Are you so sure? Is not a flag, book and effigy burnings protected forms of free speech property destruction?"

"Well, yes, I guess so. But those are special cases."

"Special Agent, we live in a time of special cases. Take the case you are working on right now. I just found out from the National

Park Service Director that one victim was Congressman Buckley of Alabama. The Director of the FBI contacted me and said that they want to make sure that nothing about this gets out on the Social Media Net. From what I gather, the FBI is planning to do some A.I. cover programming to make it look like he's still alive. Do you know why there is a DC ISB office?"

"No, sir."

"They established it at my request when I took over during the Sheppard Presidential administration. I was concerned about activities by Vice President Cordano. I was correct when Cordano became President, and I'm still concerned the problem is persisting."

"May I ask what you are concerned about?"

"You might call it moral corruption," said the Field Marshal as he leaned against the glass window. "Just watch your step with this case and send me all the file work. Don't use the main systems for this one. You are dismissed."

As Rosella was leaving the Field Marshal's office, she asked him one last question, "Sir, if I may ask? Why do you have a framed picture of Justice Sabella White on your wall? Isn't she an unsolved assassination?"

The Field Marshal responded in a monotone voice, "It reminds me of mistakes made. That will be all, Special Agent." Rosella left the Field Marshal's office in a bit of a daze about the whole thing as she returned to her cubicle. She didn't know what the Field Marshal was referring to about moral corruption. As she was lost in thought, Maurice came up to her and said, "So was it a promotion?"

"No. It was a talk about my current case," she responded in a monotone manner as she took her seat at her cubicle and pulled up her recent report. She pressed the delete button on the form, followed by entering her initials in the acknowledgment pop-up that came afterwards.

Getting up and walking by Maurice's cubicle, she said, "Maurice, if anyone asks for me, tell them I am in the field right now." "Okay, sure." Maurice said as he waved goodbye to Rosella.

IV

Rosella had her self-driving car take her to Representative Buckley's Congressional Office in the Rayburn House. From there she had the car drive to the park. Rosella downloaded the car's mapping system into her infopad and watched each street and turn. As the car drove along, she plotted DC Metropolitan Police Crime stats for the route to get a feel for an area for murders and sex crimes. It was local knowledge that those working on Capitol Hill tended to use escort services from time to time, and the stats bore out those facts with occasional charges being filed by the escorts against some Congressional Aide or worse. The funny thing was the data was showing more male escorts filing charges more than women over the years as more women entered positions of power. But she was having a hard time connecting the reported data from the First Metropolitan Police District, where the Congressional Offices were located to the Fifth Metropolitan Police District where the park was located. All the sex-murders in the Fifth District were in the Michigan Park neighborhood, not Brookland. There was a major effort to re-invent Brookland over the years, which resulted in upper scale living and lower crime. Whereas DC left Michigan Park to decay.

Rosella had the car pull over at a local Chinese restaurant she saw on route and got a small container of General Tso to go. As she ate, she continued to review the crime data on her tactical infopad. Nothing was making sense.

The car parked along Ottis Street NE bordering the park. She noticed that the crime scene tape had already been removed. The rain was letting up, turning into more of a drizzle. She got out of the car and stood next to it, looking at the modernized townhouses along Ottis Street NE.

Thinking to herself, she wiped away a strand of her red hair from her eyes. "So, Officer Ellis patrols this area. Yet there is no obvious surveillance. I don't even see the standard Police Camera systems you see scattered around this town. It is like they forgot about this park. So how is he getting his intel? Is he just camping out all night? The reports showed him coming onto the scene within at least an hour of the first two deaths. How did he know about them? What was his tip off?"

As she was getting back into the car, she saw a little girl carrying a plastic shopping bag filled with items walking towards one of the modernized townhouses.

"Now that is a vintage raincoat. You just don't see those hooded ladybug coats anymore. She must have gotten it from her grandmother."

In the spur of a moment, Rosella then on grabbed her tactical infopad from the car and ran over to the little girl. The little girl was now standing on the stoop of the townhouse. Rosella called out to her. The little girl stopped, put down the shopping bag, and turned towards Rosella.

"I am Special Agent Tolfree, and I was wondering if you could tell me if you have ever seen the following people around here before?" Rosella asked the little girl as she pulled up pics of the victims, Officer Ellis, and Troy Bentley.

The little girl pointed to Officer Ellis, Troy Bentley and Representative Buckley.

"Can you tell me when you saw them?"

In a monotone child voice, the little girl responded, "The other night entering the woods."

"Can you show me the order they entered the woods?" Asked Rosella as she pulled up the three pics.

The little girl pointed first to Representative Buckley, then Officer Ellis, followed by Troy Bentley.

"Thanks. You have been a big help. Can I visit you again if I have more questions? If need be, I can talk to your parents."

"I have only a *Birudā*, and he doesn't like company. So, I assume not." With that, the little girl picked up the bag and entered the Townhouse.

Birudā? Maybe it means uncle. The old Chinese woman who lived above my dad and I always had me call her, *Nǎinai* which is Granny. I am going to have to brush up on my Asian languages if my assignment last for more than the regular term. Rosella began to walk back to her car.

Putting her tactical pad on the passenger seat, Rosella noticed the e-message icon flashing. She opened up the app, and it was a video message from Officer Ellis.

"Hey, I thought I would let   you know you can stop investigating now. Troy Bentley just   confessed to the three murders. I arrested him earlier this   morning using a warrant I got from the FBI. He was wanted in connection with another murder down in Atlanta during a KKK rally at the Civil War Monument. DC Metropolitan is closing out the cases now that the FBI has taken Troy Bentley into custody." She closed the app, put aside the tactical infopad, and leaned back in the driver's seat. "What the fuck? Troy Bentley confessed to the three murders. The Atlanta rally murder   makes sense for a Neo-Obliteration member, but it doesn't make sense for these three murders here at this park. Unless the Neo-Obliteration movement is changing its tactics. Maybe they want their members to be more like lone wolf Jack the Rippers. Terrorizing those who support the history of the Civil War versus their normal tactics of opposing people at rallies. I know the Neo-Obliteration movement is against the Civil War, because its manifesto says it keeps hatred going on. But would they use a Jack-the-Ripper style? If that is the case, then the primary group would issue some sort of death threats or try to claim victory for the killings. But maybe this is just the first one. A sort of trial run to see if it works in theory."

Rosella tried to access the crime database to see if she could pull up Troy Bentley's record, but the local net infrastructure was poor around the park. "Dang, what is with this place. This park is a complete black hole. If I was a criminal, I would love this place. Oh, wait, someone's A-Wi-Fi hub is open in one of these townhouses. I hate to use someone else's A-Wi-Fi hub since it violates privacy laws, but this is official police work."

As she was setting up the remote access through the A-Wi-Fi hub, she noticed an active id for the U.S. Park Police on the hub. "Wait a minute, is Officer Ellis here as well? What the hell has he done?"

She pulled up the net investigation app on the tactical infopad and ran some routines to see what Officer Ellis was up to. It turned out that Officer Ellis had hacked into the house's security system and was using the door camera to watch the park. "So that is how you knew what has been going on at the park. It is not great resolution, but it beats nothing."

V

Another wave of rain started again as the sun set; Rosella sat in the car at Ottis Ave NE next to the park, reviewing Troy Bentley's records, and the filings that just occurred for the three murders, including the transcript for Troy's confession. As she downed the remaining General Tso, she told herself, "What the hell! His case has already gone through a grand jury! That's too fast for the DC U.S. Attorney's Office to process. A plea bargain! He is confessing for a plea bargain for a host of lesser charges. What the hell is up with these cases?! The confession transcript doesn't even make sense. Half of the details are a confusing jumble of facts. It wouldn't stand up in any court. Maybe the

Field Marshal is right, except the corruption has spread out to the Departments." Rosella packed it in for the night and went home. The Assistant Special Agent in Charge (ASAC) informed Rosella the next morning that the case was now being closed out by the FBI. Later that afternoon during the routine regional live video briefing, Rosella asked the Assistant Special Agent in Charge, "Sir, should I go to the protest rally being planned by the Neo-Obliteration movement in front of the United States Holocaust

Memorial Museum?"

"No, I don't think we need to be there. The US Park Police and FBI have this one."

"Are you sure? I'm very concerned with the recent news about President Jane Barker getting involved with the protests by saying that during WWII there were mistakes on both sides. I think with the recent Fort Bunker Park murders, the Neo-Obliterators maybe changing their tactics. I might get some leads at the event."

"Don't bother. I don't want us there. I suspect with the recent President's remarks, this planned protest rally by the Neo-Obliterators will be a lot more violent than the ones they have done before. The US Park Police and FBI can handle it. What I need you to pay attention to is the *Unit of Civil Enforcement* group. We are getting some intel that they are planning to set up shop in DC and other urban areas and coordinate with the Democratic National Militia people, who are already ramming cars into our monuments on the mall."

"Fine. I'll focus my resources on John Elliott's groups and coming up with some potential counter measures with local law enforcement."

"Good. Now, we need to turn our attention to a growing threat in the White Plains, NY area from the Darwinists. Ever since Texas v. Hanson, the Darwinists have been making threats;

they want to use the national monuments moved to White Plains from New York City as a keystone event for them by killing a bunch of people. Now the FBI and the US Ranger Marshals have increased their presence in the area, and I am going to assign a couple of agents to this area until this threat is resolved." The ASAC continued with the video meeting for another ten minutes.

VI

After the video meeting, Rosella didn't give the three murder cases any additional thought as she focused her attention on John Elliott's Democratic National Militia and the spin off group known as the Unit of Civil Enforcement. Both groups had been causing havoc in the Northeast Region of the ISB. The local DNM members would reprogram a self-driving car to ram into the Washington Monument or drive them into some other monument on the mall. Meanwhile, the UCE would go about the countryside enforcing its own unique brand of justice by righting local wrongs it found on the Social Media Net. According to the intel reports gathered by the FBI, the UCE was planning to recruit local DNM members to create new UCE groups to go around DC and enforce their ideals of justice. Her superiors tasked Rosella with coordinating with the local DC Metropolitan Police on developing an anti-terrorist option, since they considered the UCE to be a domestic terrorist group.

Late Thursday she got a message from the Sheriff of Pendleton County. She found some interesting "pods" out near the NSA dish area that the Sheriff thought Rosella would be interested in, so Rosella called him back that she would be out Friday to see them.

That Friday, Rosella had her driverless car take her to the Sheriff's office in Franklin, West Virginia. When Rosella went to meet the Sheriff in his office, she showed her an odd one-foot-long oblong dark plastic pod that had a flat surface on one side.

"We found about forty of the dang things up in the trees around the NSA area earlier this week." The sheriff said, leaning back in her chair with the pod sitting on his desk.

"So, where are the rest of them?"

"The FBI took the others, but I thought you might be interested in this one."

"Thanks. This might be helpful. I have seen them before, but it was about six years ago in Yellow Stone National Park on another case involving the Church of the Ember Coalition."

"Never heard of that church before." Said the Sheriff with a twang in her voice.

"I doubt you would have. They don't invite people like you or me into their inner circles." Rosella picked up the pod from the Sheriff's desk and thanked him again as she left his office.

As her car drove her back to the DC Field Office, Rosella thought, "I wonder if the weapons girls can find out something about this thing. We never got an answer about what they used them for or what they do from the FBI on the Yellow Stone Case. I thought I was done with these techno-lunatics, the Ember Coalition. I don't like the trends with the FBI and its black hole nature. We are supposed to be working together, but it seems like they are using the ISB to do grunt work."

VII

On Saturday morning, the story broke that Representative Buckley died in a private airplane crash while he was going home to Alabama. The FBI charged Troy Bentley in connection with sabotaging the airplane. Rosella was reminded of the three murders she investigated.

She sat on her love-seat, staring at the wall screen showing the crash site somewhere in North Carolina, eating her breakfast of leftovers she had in the fridge. "No way. That is not right. This is fake. But what should I do about it? Wait a minute. That means he voted in Congress this past week on that FBI bill. How could he do that if he was dead already? Oh, damn, the AI must have voted for him. No one would have known because they don't have to be on the floor to vote. Wow, I wonder how many times AIs have voted in Congress? I guess those conspiracy theorists might be right after all. The machines may run our government. But this doesn't solve the murders.

Bentley has been a scapegoat for a bigger plot. So, who did the murders?

And why make them so grisly if you just wanted to kill a congressman to secure a vote?"

Rosella picked up her tactical infopad laying on the small kitchen table in the dining alcove of her one-bedroom apartment. She began to do some research. She confirmed that Representative Buckley did vote this past week in Congress on several action items that were presented to the floor of the House of Representatives, but not anything in Committee. The system recorded him as absent for the Committee meetings. His social media accounts showed him involved with constituent comments. It was like he was never dead. Then she came across some public postings from his live-in lover he had in Georgetown, Leo Kent, this past week. Leo was asking where he was and why he wasn't returning his private messages. Then just this past Friday there was a posting from Buckley to Leo saying, "Been busy with work. Unable to get home. Must go to Alabama on a trip."

VIII

It was normal protocol to inform relatives and relations with someone's death, but there were exceptions depending upon the case. She had understood that with Representative Buckley that DC Metropolitan Police would handle this based on the file information she got, but that never happened. There was some

FBI interference on how the case was handled, although now, with the fake plane crash, she wondered if the live-in lover was aware. Rosella got dressed and went to pay Leo Kent a visit.

Her government car took her to a small condominium complex in Georgetown. According to her research, the Representative didn't own the condo, but Leo Kent did, which allowed Buckley to hide the asset and his lover, even though it was common knowledge on the Social Media Net he had a live-in lover. She approached the lobby entrance and entered Leo Kent's apartment number on the touch screen pad next to the main doors. Soon the screen was filled with an Asian man's thinly bearded face, at which point Rosella showed her badge, and said, "I am Special Agent Rosella Tolfree with the ISB. I would like to talk to you, if I may?"

"Who is the ISB? The FBI was already by this morning."

"I am part of an Investigative Branch with the Ranger Marshals."

"What do the Ranger Marshals want with me?"

"It has to do with Representative Buckley."

"Look, I already told the FBI everything this morning. It's bad enough I found out he just died in some freak airplane crash on the Social Media Net when I woke up this morning. I don't want to deal with this right now. Goodbye." And with that, the screen returned to its initial input screen.

IX

Walking back to her car, Rosella's lips narrowed as worrisome thoughts of career consequences crossed her mind. She then bit her lower lip as thoughts of a possible FBI cover up made her more upset than a loss of a promotion.

As she sat in the car, she thought to herself, "How many cover-ups have been going on with the FBI and the other departments in this city? I know we are living in some pretty chaotic political times with all the impeachments, party issues, and downright political corruption. But for departments to be affected and corrupted, groups as powerful as the FBI. I mean, everyone working in the Government has always suspected the CIA and the old NSA as being corrupt, but the FBI? Who is next, the CDC and the FDA? Maybe I should put in for a transfer back to North Central. Of course, I could end up in Alaska if I was transferred to North Central, and there have been some serious earthquakes there as of late."

She noticed the e-message app blinking on her tactical infopad and opened it up. It was a message from the DC Coroner Office with some attached reports she had requested earlier in the week when the case was active.

"They must have not gotten the message the case was closed." She said as she reviewed the reports. She continued to talk to herself as she said, "Wait a minute. Each person died due to blunt force trauma to the head with a single blow. How is that possible? What the hell? The bite marks on the genitals of the first victim are consistent with a seven-year-old dental size. A seven-year-old? Are we dealing with three people who were soliciting a minor? A minor who could smash skulls in a single blow? A seven-year- old would fit the size one woman's shoe print DC Metropolitan couldn't match up. Or is this some sort of short person fetish?

But if these reports are correct, this could mean the actual murderer is still out there, despite the FBI's attempt to cover it up. Or is this some sicko the FBI releases on the public when they need them? Okay, now I am thinking like Bruce and those wacky conspiracy theorists."

X

She instructed her car to go to her apartment, and on the way, she just sat there watching the buildings go by, thinking to herself about the idea of solicitation and the fact that Congress has a long history with escort services. "No one in Congress would ever solicit a minor because that is illegal, aside from being sick. It would be a violation of congressional ethics."

But then again, she knew of this one place when she was serving in the Pacific Field Office where there was a nudie bar, which had petite adult women for the pedophilia fanatics. "I wonder if someone is running a pedophilia fanatic escort service - but anything connected with pedophilia fanaticism is illegal on federal lands like DC. That wouldn't stop someone from trying, though."

As another rain shower began, and her car made some corrections because of an accident, she did some research about local escort services. She found many escort services, but none that would specialize in pedophilia.

She took a deeper look on the net and pulled up the net investigation app to see if it could scrape something from the wider Social Media Net. By the time she was in her apartment's underground parking garage, the app found a listing on an obscure board which seemed to be frequented by congressional staffers. In fact, there was a posting as of Friday asking if anyone was interested in a late-night hookup for this weekend. Using the investigation app she created a fake account name, and responded to the posting with a fake payment being posted to the initial poster's account. Now she waited to see if there was a response. She received a location id and the time later tonight.

"Excellent! Either I will see the murderer in question, or I am going to arrest some random person conducting an illegal pedophilia fanaticism escort service." She closed down the app and exited the car.

XI

Rosella tried to keep herself busy while she waited for the

appointed time. She did some laundry and then binge watched some old shows on the Social Media Net. She then took apart and cleaned her issued pistol, because she knew she might need it.

The location id was encoded. The car's mapping system would only reveal it upon arriving at the destination. She didn't have the time to let an app on her tactical infopad grind away at solving the location, so Rosella did not know how much travel time to allow. She figured maybe leave an hour ahead, and that's what she did. In fifteen minutes, the car parked itself along the 13th Street NE side of Fort Bunker Hill Park.

"Okay. Fort Bunker Hill."She said getting out of the car, making sure her gun was in its holster for quick access. She also pulled a tactical ear piece out of the glove compartment and placed it in her left ear. As she turned it on, she gave her employee id to the automated message. She pressed the left temple of her glasses to link the earpiece to them. A beep sounded in her ear indicating they were linked, and a small link symbol appeared in her field of view.

An ISB Agent would normally work with another ISB Agent or a Park Police Officer in such covert situations, but the DC Field Office lacked additional ISB Agents, and the local Park Police were too bureaucratic to work with, as Rosella found out when she first arrived. Rosella got used to running such covert operations by herself. She used her tactical earpiece tied into her special glasses to send a recording of the events to a backup system at HQ as a precaution.

The sun was setting, and the trees were casting long shadows, making it difficult to avoid the patches of mud in the park as she made her way up the hill. Rosella knew she was at least forty-five minutes early, but she didn't know if her perp was an early bird or not. She didn't know what she was up against. This was a risky move, and she knew it, but she couldn't call in back up for a closed-out case. All of this reminded her of her tactical basic training. When they dumped her in some wooded area with just a gun, a few rounds of paint ammo, and she had to make it to a certain point in the woods without being killed.

Rosella walked to where Representative Buckley's body was located. She stood there as the darkness set in. Rosella could see the house and streetlamps around the park from where she stood that provided some dim lighting. She made out a small person carrying a light that bounced.

As the person approached, she heard a monotone child voice call out, "Octopixy583? Are you there?"

"Yes." Rosella answered back.

As the light came close enough for Rosella to make out who was holding it, she noticed it was the little girl dressed in the vintage ladybug rain coat

"You? You are Pelicandy238?"

"Yes. I am Pelicandy238. What do you like?"

"Okay, kid, I need to know if your uncle is putting you up to this?"

"Uncle? I don't understand. Don't you want sex like the others? I am very good and know lots of sex acts."

"Doesn't '*Birudā*' mean uncle or something similar?"

"No. It is the Builder."

"Builder. What the hell are you?" Rosella said as she pulled out her pistol, pointing at the small child.

"I am a Marsha Unit. Designed to provide you with sexual pleasure. You have contracted with me to provide you with sexual pleasure tonight, and I must comply.

"You are an A-4 Pleasure unit?! But you are just a child!!"

"The other woman wanted to play with my private parts. Do you like that?"

"What? No. Tell me who your owner is?"

"*Birudā*." The small child pointed back towards the town

houses behind her.

"Can you take me to him?"

"No. I am supposed to have sex with you in the woods."

"Can I cancel the transaction?" asked Rosella.

"I don't understand," the little girl said with a puzzled look on her face as the light danced across it.

"What if I don't want to have sex with you anymore?"

"But we have done nothing? That is supposed to happen only after we have done sex acts for a while."

Putting her gun back in its holster. Rosella knelt down and began feeling around the small droid's neck and ears for a button under its thermal skin to see if she could turn the little droid unit off.

The little girl droid put down the lamp that she held and felt up Rosella's breasts, at which point Rosella stood up and backed away.

"Are you displeased? Didn't you want me to touch you back? You were touching me." The small girl asked with an inquisitive look on her face.

"Was that a sex-act for you?" Rosella asked.

"I don't understand."

"Was my touching you defined as a sex-act?"

"It can. I know sex-acts that just involve touching." The little droid responded in its girlish monotone voice. "Okay, then I am done." Rosella said.

"Are you sure? The others did a lot more. But they hurt me, so I hurt them back."

"Hurt you? How? Explain." Rosella asked.

"My head hurts when I do too many sex acts, and then I must hurt them."

"So your head hurts then you kill them?" Rosella asked as she reached for her gun.

"I don't understand kill. I hurt them, and they don't move

anymore. Then my head stops hurting."

"Did your *Birudā* make you this way?"

"No. I was always this way."

A light rain fell and could be heard hitting the fallen leaves in the woods.

"I should go since we are now done." The little girl said, picking up the lamp and turning back toward the townhouses along Ottis Ave NE.

Rosella watched the little droid so she could note the townhouse despite the dim lighting. It was the same as earlier when she was showing her the pictures of people on the stoop.

As her car drove her home from the park, she had enough evidence to pursue a raid against this *Birudā* person for operating an illegal pedophilia fanaticism service on Federal property. At least she thought so. "Does a child-size droid meet the legal tests for pedophilia?" She wondered. She grabbed her tactical info pad and looked up the laws concerning this topic. "What the? There is a specific Federal code under the pedophilia section concerning the A-4 Marsha Units? They are illegal to own and/ or operate in the U.S. and carry a minimum sentence of fifty years in prison. That's harsh. Wait, this code has been on the books for the last thirty years. That droid kid is thirty years old?! My God, how many people has it killed? I don't know who you are, Mr. *Birudā*, but you just made one serious mistake."

XII

Sunday morning Rosella went into the office. She filed an on-line Emergency Search Warrant Request with DC Magistrate Judge against 1320 Ottis Ave NE, as well as putting in for a standard Raid Request with the Ranger Marshal Unit Commander on duty. By later that afternoon all was in order, and she and a small contingent of Ranger Marshals rolled out in three armored urban troop vehicles.

Dressed in standard military armor, two Ranger Marshals busted down the front door as the rest flooded into the small townhouse. Rosella was scanning the front foyer and living room for the little girl droid and this *Birudā* person. An eclectic collection of spare droid parts and computer equipment filled the small-town house. Two of the Ranger Marshals found an old overweight man in the kitchen in the back and brought him to Rosella.

"Are you *Birudā*?" Rosella asked.

"What is going on? Who are you people?" asked the restrained and frightened old man.

"We are the Ranger Marshals, and you've violated Federal Code Section 1595d dealing with the illegal operation of an A-4 Marsha Unit, as well as Federal Code Section 1252c concerning operating an illegal pedophilia fanaticism service on Federal lands. Where is the droid, sir."

"But Marsha is a collector's item. It took months for me to acquire her from Japan. You can't take her from me. She is a crown jewel of a droid."

"Take him out of here. The droid must be here somewhere. Just don't touch it."

In her helmet, Rosella heard one of the Ranger Marshals say they found the droid unit in the basement. Rosella proceeded to the basement and found three Ranger Marshals with their weapons trained on the little girl droid huddled in the basement's corner.

"Do you remember me from last night?" Rosella asked. "Yes. You are Octopixy583."

"That's right. Now would you come with me?" Rosella asked, holding out her hand to the droid.

"Do you want to have sex again?"

"Yes. Why don't you come with me, and these men outside?"

"Are they wanting to have sex with me as well? I am programmed for multiple partner sex-acts."

"Maybe. Let's just go upstairs and outside to the park, okay?"

"Okay." The little girl droid said as she walked up the stairs out of the basement.

As they were exiting the townhouse, the little girl said to Rosella, "Why is the door broken?"

Not knowing what to say, Rosella said, "Something happened to it."

As the droid, Rosella and three Ranger Marshals were walking across the street, the droid asked, "Where is *Birudā*?"

"He's at the store." Rosella said as a quick response. "But he doesn't like to go outside. I don't understand."

"Well, this time he had to get some medicine." Rosella said, trying to keep the droid focused.

"But he is not sick. I don't understand," said the little droid as it turned around to walk back to the townhouse.

"We are not at the park yet. I still want to have sex." Rosella said to the droid to coax it to the park.

"I need to find *Birudā*. I need to confirm the transaction," the small droid girl said as her eyes darted back and forth as she turned her head back and forth.

Just then the little girl droid spotted the old man being shoved into one of the armored urban troop vehicles with his wrists bound behind his back.

"*Birudā*. You are hurting *Birudā*. Error 295. Error 295. Error 295. Error 295. Error 295. " The little droid kept saying as it stood there motionless.

"Tactical, what the hell is an A-4 Error 295?" Rosella asked through her built-in helmet comm.

"Hold on. That's an old error code. The database says it is the safety protocols of the built-in fusion systems. Ma'am, I think we are dealing with a potential fusion explosion."

"Shit! Are you detecting any micro-Graviton waves?"

"No, Ma'am."

Recalling her training on A-4 fusion systems, if there were no micro-Graviton waves detected then it was safe to shut down the unit and not risk a fusion explosion. Pulling out her pistol, Rosella shot the small droid in the head, blowing it clean off, and with that the little droid's body collapsed backwards with the force of the gunshot.

"Bag it up." She told the three Ranger Marshals that were with her.

XIII

Monday late afternoon, the {Field Marshal} {insert name } requested Rosella's presence.

Rosella entered his office on the seventh floor, dressed as professional as she could be. The Field Marshal was already sitting at his desk. He waved at her to sit. Rosella took a seat in one of the two chairs in front of his desk.

"Congratulations on taking down that illegal Marsha unit, Special Agent Tolfree. You took an enormous risk going solo, but I'm glad everything worked out." The Field Marshal paused, and then continued, "I have been reviewing your career file. You appear to have been transferred around a lot. Do you have troubles with co-workers?"

"No, Sir. I guess I'm more of a loner than a group player."

"I see. Well, the work you did this past weekend was excellent. Customs is still trying to figure out how this Rudolph Hilprand got an illegal A-4 unit into this country. Is there anything else I should know before I dismiss you?"

"Sir, I'm concerned about the FBI."

"In what way?"

"Representative Buckley voted on floor items when he was in fact dead."

"I see." The Field Marshal paused, leaned back in his chair and continued to say, "You should know Rudolph Hilprand, the man you arrested, has been taken into custody by the FBI this afternoon along with the remains of the A-4 Marsha unit. The FBI is taking over the pedophilia case against him in cooperation with the U.S. Attorney's Office for DC."

"What? The FBI already wrongly charged Troy Bentley with the Congressman's murder. Hilprand would be guilty of the murder being the owner of the android. I was planning to process the paperwork for the U.S. Attorney's Office to charge Hilprand instead." Rosella stated.

Still leaning back in his chair, the Field Marshal said after breathing out a sigh, "I'm afraid your report will have to neglect those details for now. I also don't want you to process any paperwork charging Hilprand with the murder of the Congressman. Hilprand was just operating an illegal A-4 unit, and that's all. Do you understand, Special Agent Tolfree?"

"Yes, sir. But begging your pardon, why are we letting the FBI get away with this one?"

"I have my reasons. That's all you need to know, Special Agent. You're dismissed."

Rosella got up and left the Field Marshal's office. As she returned to her cubicle, she wondered what was going on in DC with the FBI. She liked none of it. It felt wrong to her sense of justice. When she worked in other ISB field offices, the FBI and the Park Police were more helpful, but everything with DC was not like that. Everyone seemed so protective of their own dominions, with no desire to help you unless it benefited them in some manner. "It was no wonder they moved the ISB Headquarters outside DC when they made the Ranger Marshals," Rosella thought to herself.

#   #   #   #   #

BLOG EXCERPT

From www.RosellaTolfree.com, blog entry entitled
"Character Notes of Rosella Tolfree" posted on 10-8-2021.

Her Early Life

Born 19 years before the Presidency of Rick Garrett and 20 years before the formation of the Ranger Marshals. She grew up as a child during the late Economic Isolationist Recovery Period, when America was recovering from the twin disasters of the Great Melt and the New Madrid Volcanic Traps. America had turned inward, like many nations. And focused on rebuilding itself. A period of omnibus legislation to deal with issues and reconstruct society materially. It's also a time of disillusionment with the government and society, as people did things to take care of themselves first and didn't care about others. This despite the technological wonders about them, such a fusion power.

Childhood

Rosella lived with her father, Mordell Tolfree, in the remodeled landscape of San Francisco, California. As a child, she could see the remains of parts of old skyscrapers sticking out of the water. She would see people working on them to recover whatever scrap they could, but by her time they had picked clean many, leaving the salt water to corrode the remains. Many of the old buildings became roosting sites for My Pet Dragons. A genetically altered lizard turned into a model flying mini dragon. One of humanity's genetic mistakes that got away from us. It occupied the same ecological niche of birds and resulted in the extinction of many wild bird species. She would watch these small flying lizards trying to catch fish.

Like all children of her time, she attended on-line schooling. She did very well in school and had an innate aptitude to apply herself. She would do her schoolwork with precision and helped around the house with chores. But with her own room, it was always a mess. Even today, as an adult, she leaves a mess in her government car while keeping other areas in her life nice and neat.

One odd thing for Rosella was she never got sick as a child. Despite the availability of free medical services, her father never used them for her. Except once when he took her to the dentist at the urging of a teacher. The dentist said she had the most perfect teeth and gums she had ever seen in a child.

Unlike the other kids in the neighborhood who got vaccines for childhood illnesses, she didn't, but she never got sick either. No colds, no allergies, and scratches healed up with no issues. Oddly, she could eat foods that most people would consider past its prime. This turned into contests with her on-line classmates in middle school, where they would dare each other to eat stuff left out too long. Rosella always won and earned the nickname Rosella Iron Belly.

Teen Years

Being a cloned female, Rosella's genes and anatomy were altered. Genetically puberty was delayed until closer to her mid-teens. This was true for all cloned females. A cloned female would have growth spurts and other changes starting around 14 to 15 years of age that lasted until the age of 19. Going through all "Tanner Stages" in this period. Which, for normally conceived humans, would typically end at 15 years of age. As a result, cloned females socially enjoyed a longer childhood. This is not true for cloned males who matured at the normal rates because of the lack of altered anatomy and genes.

During this time of changes, Rosella became extremely irritable around her father. The smallest thing would set her off, causing her to retreat to her room, slamming the door. It sounds like typical teenage behavior, but for her father, his little girl was now insane and uncontrollable. In her late high school years, she became on-line friends with fellow students her father disapproved of because of the type of video games they played and their general anti-social nature. Despite all this behavior, her grades never suffered, and she was still pulling a straight 4.0.

It all reminded her father of his drug dealing days, and the behavior of a bad junky. When he got a chance, he would check her room for drugs in all the common hiding places he knew. He even installed dark programs on her computer to monitor her activities. He found nothing, and as quickly as this started, the behavior ended. It was gone when she turned 18 and was going off to college.

What's it like being a Female Clone?

The android that created Rosella made her without a uterus. This is an unresolved "bug" with the A-4 birthing androids. She, like all female clones, still has her ovaries.

The "bug" was discovered after the A-4 birthing androids were introduced and began producing female children. Without a uterus and the ovaries still present, this caused ovarian failure. Which led to a collapse of puberty factors. As a result, these initial children ended up being child sized women and lacked adult female features.

Once discovered, they sent a genetic patch out that still allowed female puberty patterns to occur despite the lack of a uterus and presence of ovarian collapse. Albeit they delayed the puberty patterns in age.

This situation causes a host of long-term medical problems from general irritability to profound fatigue, to loss of sexual desire and other issues with sexuality and associated pleasure, insomnia, anxiety, suicidal thoughts, nervousness, to even more minor issues like muscles, joint or bone pains and headaches.

For Rosella, when she was in her late teen years, she was very irritable and battled with insomnia. The problem of insomnia continues today and resulted in her developing sexsomnia while in college. After her father's death, she had trouble socializing and once she was transferred to the Washington, D.C. office, she lost interest in interacting with people outside traditional work. These losses of socialization and interaction caused her to be more alone and isolated from other people.

Conspiracy theorists on the Social Media Net speculate that they did this puberty delay because of involvement by the Church of the Ember Coalition. They point to a group of wealthy women, who were members of the Church, that were publicly advocating genetically delaying female puberty to reduce teen pregnancy.

#   #   #   #   #

LIST OF OTHER

ROSELLA TOLFREE STORIES

Rosella Tolfree's Mother's Day

A story that won the weekly Reedsy short story contest and started the whole Rosella Tolfree world, can be found on Medium at https://medium.com/reedsy/rosella-tolfrees-mother-s-day-b70ef1cf9492

As well as in the paperback version of Volume 4. This short story tells of the nature of Rosella's birth, her early childhood, and about the unsolved murder of her father. She is 43 when this story takes place.

Seth Underwood's Medium Page

Rosella Gets Her First Tattoo, and It's Medical. A short story about the future of tattoos and how A.I. is involved. Rosella is 19 years of age in this story. It can be found at https://medium.com/data-driven-fiction/the-future-of-tattooing-maybe-programmable-f4a1a231c7cc

www.rosellatolfree.com

You will find an ongoing blog providing background details and commentary. Not to mention links and where there is more in depth explanations of world dynamics, plus other historical peoples and events.

USRM-ISB Installment 0.43 - April Fools

This is a short short story (including a YouTube video) that's an April Fools joke played on Rosella by a co-worker. Rosella is 43 in this story. It can be found at https://www.rosellatolfree.com/home/usrm-isb-installment-043-april-fools

Rosella Tolfree World Stories on the E-JSD on Substack

The Story of Thomas Finley
The Story of Cory Sheppard

CHECK OUT OUR OTHER VOLUMES

Volume 1

Seth Underwood offers to us a small collection of future events, and two short stories involving his female android science fiction. In the story, "The A-4 known as Helen", his model A-4 Android contracts a disease and with his story, "The Pallas Quarantine", there is a love relationship between a human female and an A-4 Android.

Volume 2

Emmett Gray gives us with two of his science fiction short stories. One dealing man's first mission to Mars that is actually more like a game show, and how part of mankind is dealing with Earth's destiny with asteroid 2080B.

Volume 3

Again Seth Underwood presents his ongoing storytelling and explanation of possible future historical events involving the crisis looming from melting of the ice caps due to Global Warming. Included in this volume is his story entitled "The Poverty Revolt of Titan" when humanity has colonized the planets.

Volume 4

T. S. Dickson provides us with two of his general fiction short stories. Lose yourself in two brooding, introspective, and thought-provoking works of speculative fiction of a rising literary star.

VISIT OUR WEBSITE
to see the latest available reads

https://www.josephstreetdigest.com

https://www.e-jsd.page/

LIKE US ON SOCIAL MEDIA

Facebook
https://www.facebook.com/JosephStreetDigest

Instagram
https://www.instagram.com/joseph.street.digest

Twitter
https://twitter.com/JosephStDigest

MORE ABOUT
ROSELLA TOLFREE'S WORLD
CAN BE FOUND AT

WWW.ROSELLATOLFREE.COM

BLOG POSTS ABOUT ROSELLA'S WORLD
AND MORE...

Maeve, the Psycho A-4 Android

www.ingramcontent.com/pod-product-compliance
Lightning Source LLC
Chambersburg PA
CBHW010348220726
48290CB00016B/2679